To Daniel Stokes

My name is Gaia Moore, I'm seventeen years old, and for the first time I can remember, no one is trying to kill me.

I know what you're thinking: I'm a schizophrenic paranoid delusional. This is not a normal thing for a seventeen-year-old girl to say. But that's just it. I'm not a normal seventeen-year-old girl. I wasn't normal at fifteen or ten. The last time I remember knowing that I was safe was when I was about eight, making mud pies in the backyard in the Berkshires, my knees covered in Rugrats Band-Aids. But even then I wasn't safe—I just didn't know it yet.

I've never had a normal life, and that's all I ever wanted.

I wanted afternoons filled with soccer practice instead of tactical training. I wanted my mother to live long enough to hear about my first kiss. I wanted a father who was around to read me bedtime stories every night instead of disappearing for days at a time. All I wanted was an existence that even vaguely resembled those of the well-adjusted ballerinas and spelling-bee champions and hopscotch experts around me.

But I could never have that. Someone in my family was always in danger. Someone was always trying to kidnap me or experiment on me or—you know—kill me. My mother was murdered. My father has been presumed dead more times than I can remember. I've had friends beaten and shot and stabbed. My first boyfriend almost died because of me.

Nothing was ever normal. Until now.

This is what normal feels like. I don't have to sit around wondering what Loki's going to do next, because he's gone—buried somewhere inside my uncle Oliver's subconscious. I don't have to spend my time trying to think like Natasha or Tatiana to figure out their strategy, because they're in custody. We still don't know who kidnapped my dad and took him to Russia, but the CIA is working on it, and for now, he's home. With me. Me and Dad, living together, alone. Like we're supposed to be. Like a family.

So there's no reason to obsess. No reason to plan and plot and chase and spy. I don't even have to train. I don't *have* to do anything.

This is what normal feels like.

I don't know what to do with myself.

To: Y
From: X22
Subject: Prisoner 352, Codename Abel

There has been a security breech in sub-sector K. Prisoner 352 is AWOL. Unconfirmed reports state that a young woman, believed to be Genesis, along with two men were instrumental in the liberation of 352/Abel. They are believed to be en route to the States, if not already there. We await your orders.

All is well,
Gaia thought,
taking a deep
breath. She
almost didn't **a**
dare to **perfect**
believe
it, but **moment**
it was
true.

GAIA MOORE WAS HAVING A MOMENT

she'd probably remember for-ever. She was one of those rare people who had these burned-in-her-memory moments all the time, but this one was dif-ferent.

"So, listen . . ."

This one was good.

Good memorable moments were atypical in Gaia's particularly screwed-up life. The awful ones, those came up all the time.

Like the moment she learned her mother was dead. The moment she realized that the man she had always thought was her father might actually be her evil uncle, Loki. The moment Mary passed away. The moment Sam was kidnapped. The moment that Loki operative fired shots at Ed. The list of gut-wrenching, miserable, devastating moments went on and on.

But these light, content, all-is-right-with-the-world moments? They were very few and very far between. And when she realized she was having one, instead of automatically thinking of the few things that were still wrong—things that could crap all over the moment like a giant pigeon—Gaia just smiled.

For once she was going to let herself be happy.

"I like this," Jake Montone said, lying back next to her on the big mound of rock near the Columbus

Circle entrance to Central Park. "Who would've thought there was actually a place in this city where you could see stars? Actual ones, I mean. Famous people I've been seeing everywhere lately. It's like you get one warm day and they suddenly come out of hiding. I was almost nailed by Brad Pitt on Rollerblades this afternoon in Union Square."

"Jake?" Gaia said, the back of her skull searching for a smooth bit of stone to rest on.

"Yeah?" he asked. He turned his head so he was looking at her profile.

"Shut up," she said.

"Right."

Ever since Gaia, Jake, and Oliver had returned from their little `smash-and-grab job` in the former Soviet Union (they'd smashed a fortress and grabbed Gaia's dad, Tom), Jake had been prone to these little fits of verbosity. Just every once in a while. Like he was a little kid that was still psyched up by a trip to an amusement park and couldn't contain his excitement. Gaia would never admit it, but somewhere deep down she kind of thought it was cute. In an irritating sort of way.

A jagged point bit into the back of her head and she moved again, sighing in frustration. Jake sat up, slipped out of his denim jacket, bunched it into a ball, and moved to prop it under the back of her head. For a split second Gaia thought about refusing, making a crack about his chivalry and turning it into a joke, but she stopped herself. Instead she just lifted her head, then leaned back into the Jake-scented softness.

Ah. Pillow. Just one more thing to make the perfect moment last.

All is well, Gaia reflected again, taking in another deep breath. She almost didn't dare to believe it, but it was true. Her father was home, safe and sound. Her uncle had been living for days now as good old normal Uncle Oliver with no signs of Loki-ness whatsoever. There was no one out there hunting her down, tracking her every move, plotting ways to take her out.

And to top it all off, she had a new friend. A real friend. Surprisingly enough Jake Montone had turned out to be, contrary to all snap judgments, a non-moron. He was, in fact, `freakishly true`. Supportive. Noble almost.

"I can't believe that guy actually gets to have sex with Jennifer Aniston," he said suddenly, his brow furrowing beneath his tousled dark hair.

Okay, so he was also still a guy. But he had already saved Gaia's life, accepted her increasingly psychotic family situation with only pertinent questions asked, *and* dropped everything to come to Russia with her to save her father. In a short time he'd gone beyond the call of duty, friendship-wise. He'd gone beyond the call of duty for a damn guardian angel.

"So, anybody at school ask where you were for the past few days?" Jake asked.

"Not really. The teachers are used to me disappearing, and no one else in the world notices."

Except Sam, Gaia thought, her heart giving an extra-hard thump. *Sam noticed.* Sam had noticed to the tune of eight messages on her answering machine. Gaia had been more than a little surprised when she heard his voice over and over and over again on the tape. The last time she'd seen the guy he'd basically told her to get out of his life and stay out. By the time she was done listening to his messages it was fairly clear that he wanted the exact opposite.

I need to call him back, Gaia thought. But even as her brain formed the suggestion, the rest of her felt exhausted by the mere thought. The last thing she wanted right now was to open a can of emotionally wrought worms. She'd much rather just stay where she was—lying on her back in the park, staring at the sky, with Jake's warmth next to her, keeping the goose bumps at bay.

"What about your dad?" Gaia asked. Jake had been staying with Oliver since their return from Russia. Oliver needed to make sure no one was watching Jake's building. There was no way Jake's father was still buying any "I'm just staying at a friend's/there's a last minute school trip/my dog ate my homework" excuses any longer.

"Luckily Dad had to go out of town for some physicians' conference," Jake said. "He left before I got back and he doesn't even realize I haven't been home." He pulled his tiny cell out of the front pocket of his jeans and checked the screen. "The beauty of the cell phone."

"Nice," Gaia said.

"Besides, Oliver says I can go back tonight," Jake told her, replacing the phone after scrolling through a few text messages. "He gave the all clear."

"I'm glad," Gaia said sincerely.

"So, listen," Jake said, propping himself up on his elbow and turning on his side.

Gaia swallowed and her stomach turned. It was a loaded "so listen." The kind that was usually followed by either an unpleasant announcement like, "So, listen, I'm moving to Canada." Or by an awkward-silence-inducing question like, "So, listen, do you want to go to the prom?" Not that Gaia had ever been asked to a prom before, but she could still identify the appropriate `"so, listen."`

She stared at the sky and held her breath, waiting for the ax to fall, not sure of which ax would be the quicker, less painful one. Gaia had been getting the `more-than-a-friend vibe` from Jake for a few days now, but she'd chosen to ignore it. Mostly because acknowledging it would require acknowledging the fact that she was also attracted to him and Gaia was definitely not ready to go there.

10

Not just yet.

Whenever she allowed herself to admit she liked a guy, only anguish ensued.

"I was wondering if you might want to—"

Jake's question was interrupted by a sudden, blinding light that was directed right into his eyes. He held up his hand to shield himself and the beam moved to Gaia's face. She squinted against the stinging pain and sat up, her boots scraping against the grainy surface of the rock.

"What do you kids think you're doing out here at this hour?" an authoritative voice asked.

The light finally moved away and Gaia was able to distinguish the outlines of two NYC police officers through the pink dots that were floating across her vision.

"Just hanging out," Jake said, pushing himself to his feet. He was slightly taller and more than slightly broader than either of the men in blue.

"Yeah, well, it's not the safest place to *just hang out* these days," the chubbier of the two cops said, eyeing Gaia as she stood. He shone his light along the ground, looking for beer cans, crushed joints—anything that could allow him to give more than the usual amount of hassle to Jake and Gaia.

"We've had a number of attacks in this area of the park in the past few days," Cop Number One said. "I suggest you two move it along, for your own safety."

"Sure," Jake said, leaning down to grab his jacket. "No problem, Officer."

He used his jacket to nudge Gaia's arm and they turned and scrambled down the side of the boulder. Gaia sighed as she fought for her footing on the steep side of the rock. She appreciated what the cops were trying to do, but they'd obliterated her perfect moment. Of course, they may have also saved her from an awkward, embarrassing, tongue-tied conversation with Jake about his "so, listen." Little did they know they'd just added `"rescue from ill-fated romantic interludes"` to their duties as New York's finest.

Gaia jumped the last few feet to the ground and landed next to Jake. He shoved his arms into his jacket and straightened the collar as they started to walk. For a few blissful seconds there was total silence—aside from the faint honking of car horns somewhere out on the streets that surrounded the park.

Then, Jake tried again. "So, anyway, as I was saying—"

"Hey! No! Help! *Help!*"

It took Gaia a split second to realize that she wasn't hearing her own desperate get-me-out-of-here pleas, but actual shouts of panic.

"It's coming from over there," Jake said, taking off.

Gaia was right at his heels, slicing through toward what sounded like a struggle. They suddenly emerged into a small clearing and saw not one, but two middle-aged women in jogging suits, flattened on their backs by four men in jeans and do-rags. Two of the men were each holding a woman down and two of the men were yanking at each of their clothes.

Gaia took one look at the tearstained and desperate face of the woman closest to her and felt her fingers curl into fists.

"Hey!" Jake shouted at the top of his lungs.

All four men stopped and whipped their heads around. At the instant of surprise, Jake and Gaia both launched themselves at the clothing-gropers and tackled them off their victims. As Gaia tumbled head over heels with her man, she saw the two women struggle to their feet.

"Go!" Gaia told them, flipping the assailant over and digging one knee into his back. A second guy wrapped his arm around her and yanked her off his friend. "Get out of here!" she screamed at the joggers.

The stunned, shaken women seemed to come to at that moment and they wisely ran. Gaia was thrown away from her second man and she had to fight for her balance. As soon as she found her footing again, she got her game face on. Jake was working his best *Matrix*-worthy moves on his two guys as Gaia's men circled, leering at her.

"We got the girl, Slick," one of them said, punctuating his statement by spitting at her feet. "Aren't we lucky?"

Slick looked Gaia up and down slowly. "You said it, buddy."

If you're feeling so lucky, come and get me, Gaia thought. *Quit wasting my time.*

Slick came at her then with a clumsy one-two punch, which she easily blocked. She thrust the heel of her hand up into his nose, waited for the satisfying crack and the `spurt of blood`, then turned around, hoisted him onto her back and over her shoulder. He landed on the ground in front of her, clutching his nose, rolling back and forth and groaning in pain.

Gaia looked up at his friend and lifted her eyebrows. "Ready?"

He let out a growl and ran at her. Gaia was about to throw a roundhouse at him when Jake shouted her name. She looked up at the last second and saw a third guy coming at her from her left. Glancing at their trajectories, Gaia quickly ducked, crouching as low to the ground as possible. She smiled when she heard the *thwack,* then stood up and slapped her hands together.

Both of the thugs were laid out on the ground, unconscious. They'd smacked heads coming at her and knocked themselves out. It was almost too easy.

"Amateurs," Gaia said under her breath, stepping over one of the bodies.

"Nice work," Jake told her, reaching out his hand. They high-fived and Gaia noticed that the fourth guy was also unconscious, crumpled into a seated position against a tree.

"You, too," she said.

They looked up when they heard rustling in the dark and the huffing and puffing of approaching men. The two cops that had roused them from the boulder came skidding into the clearing, hands on their holsters. They took one look around at the men on the ground, then gazed at Gaia and Jake, stunned.

"What happened here?" Chubby Cop asked, looking impressed against his will. "I thought we told you two to move along."

"And we did," Jake said, opening his arms. "You're welcome."

Cop Number Two shot Jake a wry smile as he knelt down to cuff Slick. "And now you can hang out while we get your statements, wise guy," he said.

Gaia and Jake exchanged a quick smile and leaned back against a thick tree trunk to wait. The side of Gaia's shoulder pressed into the back of Jake's and she didn't move away.

"They're gonna take credit for this, aren't they?" Jake whispered.

"Probably," Gaia replied.

"Figures. I feel like Batman. I keep kicking ass and there's no one I can tell about it," Jake said. Then he smiled and nudged his shoulder back into hers. "'Cept you."

Gaia felt the corners of her mouth tugging up slightly. What was wrong with her? Was she actually *enjoying* flirtation?

"So, Gray's Papaya after this?" Jake asked as the

cops roused the two knuckleheads that had run into each other.

Gaia's stomach grumbled. "Definitely."

She tucked her chin and turned her face away from him, smiling for real. She'd been doing this forever—beating up toughs in the park, ducking from or dealing with cops, then going for a post-fight midnight snack. But she'd been doing it forever alone. And she'd always thought that was the way she liked it. Yes, actually. That was the way she *had* liked it.

But now. . . now she liked having someone there. She liked having Jake to share all this with. She liked having an. . . ally.

Huh. Maybe it's true, Gaia thought, an evening breeze tickling a few strands of her long blond hair against her face. *Maybe things* can *change.*

TOM MOORE SAT AT THE SMOOTH

metal table and glared across at the prisoners. His spine was straight, his fingers clasped into a knot, his elbows just slightly off the edge of the table-

Venom

top. He breathed in and out deliberately, maintaining his composure—maintaining his calm.

Just another set of criminals. Just another day.

"Are you going to say anything?" Natasha asked.

"I'll ask the questions," Tom spat back instantly. He could taste the venom in his own mouth.

Just another set of criminals. Just another day.

Tatiana blinked but remained otherwise impassive. She looked small and wan, her light skin translucent and green in her bright orange jumpsuit. The monstrous cuffs circling her tiny wrists were almost comical. Even though it was impossibly cold in the interrogation room, there was a line of sweat visible above her upper lip. It was taking a lot more effort for Tatiana to remain composed after days of stony, obstinate silence in her cell. Far more effort than her more experienced, more world-weary, more spy-game–weary mother.

Tom shifted his gaze to Natasha again. Her dark hair was pulled back in a low braid that hung heavy and smooth down her back. She wore an amused smirk on her face. The face he had once held, once kissed, once touched with the tenderness that he'd formerly reserved only for his wife—his one true love.

An acidic bitterness shot through his stomach. He could only hope his nausea couldn't be detected by the detainees.

"That's fine," Natasha said finally, shifting slightly in her iron chair. "It's just that you're not. Asking questions, that is."

"For whom were you working?" Tom asked flatly.

17

The smirk deepened. "You don't want to know that, Tom."

"Don't say my name," he snapped. "You don't have that right."

Maddeningly, the smirk turned into a smile.

"For whom were you working?" he repeated.

"Everything is connected, Tom," Natasha said lightly. "It's all coming full circle."

"Oh, so now we're being cryptic," Tom snapped.

"You have to see the bigger picture. You have to look to the past to clearly see the future."

Tom clenched his teeth. She was trying to make him think about Katia, trying to make him crack. But Katia was not just his past. She was his past, his present, his future. Why he'd ever let himself lose sight of that, he had no idea.

"For whom were you working?" Tom repeated once again, glaring at her.

"I want to talk about a deal," she said.

Tom got up and threw his chair across the room, the noise slicing his eardrums as it clattered and crashed. Tatiana flinched as he leaned his knuckles into the table and got right in Natasha's face.

"You tried to kill my daughter! You tried to *kill* Gaia! And you have the audacity. . . the unmitigated *gall* to sit here and talk to me about a *deal!?*" he shouted, his eyes so wide they felt about to burst.

She didn't move. She didn't blink. And suddenly

Tom Moore knew. He knew that he was going to grab her. He saw his hands around her throat. Saw himself choking the life out of her. Who would blame him if he did it? The woman was sitting here talking in code, making up riddles, and she'd tried to murder the only family he had left. She deserved to die.

"Agent Moore!"

The door to the cinderblock-walled room flew open and Director Vance stood on the threshold, his intimidating former–Navy Seal, former–NCAA basketball player frame blocking out the light from the hallway. He pressed his full lips together into a thin line.

"That's enough, Agent Moore," Vance said in his rumbling baritone.

Tom didn't move. His knuckles turned white against the table as he continued to glare into Natasha's unwavering eyes.

I told this person I loved her. I thought I was going to be with her forever, he thought. The visions he'd had of himself and Natasha together—of making a family with their daughters—flitted through his mind, whirling together in a sickening tornado of colors.

"Agent Moore, I'm not going to ask you again," Vance said, stepping into the room.

The whirlwind suddenly stopped. Tom swallowed hard and struggled to focus on Vance. Ever so slowly, some semblance of balance returned to his mind and he realized what he was doing. He was letting Natasha get the upper hand. He was letting her have the whole game. He smoothed down the front of his blue suit jacket, hoping to regain some shred of dignity.

But when he glanced at her again it was clear from the expression of triumph on her face that all was lost. He couldn't handle being around her. And he'd just proven it.

Tom turned and followed his director out of the room and into the monitoring space just beyond. A couple of agents stood in front of the one-way glass that looked over the interrogation room and they averted their eyes when Tom entered. The second the door was shut behind him, Vance turned on Tom, his dark eyes livid, his deep brown skin flushed with anger.

"Moore, don't you *ever* let me see you lose your cool like that with a prisoner again, you understand me?" Vance spat, leaning in over Tom. "You know what you were in that room? You were that prisoner's bitch!"

Tom pulled his head back slightly, unaccustomed to such severe scolding after his glorious tenure in the CIA. Still, he knew on some level that Vance was right. There wasn't much he could say.

"I'm sorry, sir," he said, swallowing his pride. "It won't happen again."

"Damn right it won't. Because you're going home," Vance said through his teeth.

It took Tom more time than absolutely necessary to process this. The man couldn't be suggesting that he was being taken off this case. Didn't Vance know how invested in this he was? He had to find out who had kidnapped him, who had ordered his daughter to be killed. He had to find out for sure whether or not his brother, Oliver, was involved as he so highly suspected.

"What?" Tom spat out finally. "No! Sir, I—"

"You heard me, Moore," Vance said. "These particular prisoners obviously have you more than a little on edge." He paused for a breath and looked at Tom sorrowfully, almost pityingly. "You're taking a little time off," he added, causing Tom's heart to sink with the finality of it all. "Starting now."

Out with the Old . . .

GAIA OPENED THE DOOR TO THE 72nd Street apartment on Friday after school and immediately went on alert. There was a crash coming from Natasha's—no, her *father's*—bedroom. She and Jake looked at each other. There was someone else there.

Her first instinct was to call her father's name and see if it was him. But what if it was an intruder? Then she'd just end up calling attention to herself and Jake. Gaia tiptoed toward the living room, her rubber-soled boots soundless on the hardwood floor.

Footsteps approached, confident and loud and not remotely trying to be stealthy. Gaia flattened herself against the nearest wall, around the corner from the hallway. That was when her father emerged into the room, all smiles.

"Hey, honey!" he said, shuffling a few envelopes in his hands. His dress shirt was unbuttoned at the top and the sleeves were rolled up above his wrists. "I didn't hear you come in!"

His eyes flicked to Jake, who was now standing outside the door to the kitchen, his muscles visibly slackening.

"Hello, Jake," Tom said as Gaia forced her fingers and her jaw to unclench.

Her father breezed by her and sat down at the head of the dining room table where there were dozens of neatly arranged piles of bills and papers. He started pulling papers out of the envelopes, sorting them, and tossing the envelopes into the kitchen garbage can.

Gaia eyed her father. This was all very weird. Not only was he home in the middle of the day, but he was doing paperwork—something she hadn't seen him do. . . ever. When her mom was alive, that was her territory, and since then her father had never been around for enough days in a row to even know that there *were* bills.

On top of it all, there was an odd air about him. He was humming. His knee was bouncing under the table. Her father was normally cool, aloof, sometimes intense, but always in a quiet way. Just then he was acting, well, hyper.

"Dad?" Gaia asked, tucking her hair behind her ears. "Everything okay?"

"Fine. Great, actually," he said, glancing up at her for a split second before returning his attention to the papers.

Jake moved into the room, stuffing his hands into the front pockets of his jeans and giving Tom a wide berth. Gaia could tell that Jake sensed something was up.

"I heard a crash in the bedroom," Gaia said, sitting down in a chair across from her father. She pulled her messenger bag off over her head and laid it on the floor.

"Right, I broke a lamp," her father said. "I'll clean it up later."

Gaia looked at Jake and he tilted his head, giving her a look that said, *"He's your father."*

"Okay, so what are you doing home?" Gaia asked, glancing at her black plastic watch. "It's four o'clock."

"I decided to take some time off," Tom said, slapping a piece of paper down on top of a pile. Her father taking time off? Was this some kind of new, previously unexplored reality?

"What? But Dad, what about Natasha and Tatiana? What about your kidnappers? You can't just—"

23

"But I am," he said calmly. "My director thinks I need to take a break and I agree."

He was lying. She could tell by the way his jaw was tensing, making his cheek bulge slightly. He didn't want to take time off—his director was making him. This was insane. How were they supposed to find out who had kidnapped him if they weren't even going to let him interrogate the two people who *might* give them a lead?

"We're both going to have to let the CIA do their job," her father said, reading her distraught expression perfectly.

Gaia had no idea how he could be so accepting of this. Her father wasn't a quitter; he was a fighter—just like her. She wasn't going to just drop this investigation. She'd do it on her own if she had to, no matter what the CIA or her father said. Whoever had kidnapped her father had to be found and be brought to justice.

"In the meantime there's something I wanted to talk to you about," her father said with a forced smile. "How would you feel about making a new start?"

"What kind of new start?" Gaia asked slowly, still adjusting to his new attitude.

"Should I—" Jake asked, motioning toward the bedrooms.

"No, stay," Tom said with a laugh. "I just wanted to ask Gaia if she'd like to do a little shopping this weekend."

Gaia's jaw dropped, but she recovered quickly and snapped it shut again. That was definitely a phrase she never thought she'd hear. Not from her father, anyway. The things she heard most often from him were phrases like, "Stay off the radar," "I'll try to be in touch sometime next month," and "Aim for the solar plexus."

"Shopping?" Gaia asked, slumping back in her seat. "For what?"

Please don't let him say bras or something like that, Gaia thought. *Like he suddenly wants to make up for not being there and for my not having a mother.*

Gaia didn't blame her father for his many disappearing acts over the years—at least not anymore—not now that she knew what he was doing on all those excursions and why. He was fighting the good fight. Protecting her. Protecting the free world. It had taken Gaia a long time to accept that and move on. She couldn't handle it if he decided to take on the role of guilt-ridden father now.

"New furniture," Tom said. "Everything in this place belongs to Natasha and Tatiana. I think it's time we get some of our own things, don't you?"

A little stirring of excitement came to life in Gaia's chest, quelling the determination for revenge ever so slightly. She hadn't thought of it that way, but her father was right. This place was going to be their home. Their home. She and her father hadn't had one of those in years. Why would they want it to be decorated by their evil archenemy?

"Really?" Gaia said, too unaccustomed to the idea of doing something as normal as furniture shopping with her father.

"Yes, really," Tom said, standing. He moved over to the end of the hallway and looked off toward the opposite end—toward the room Gaia once shared with Tatiana. "We can get rid of those two beds and get you a double. . . move out that old-fashioned desk—I'm guessing it's not your style," he added with a grin.

Gaia liked what he was saying, but the way he was saying it was still odd. Almost manic. He was too excited about the prospect of shopping.

He wants to be at work, she thought with total certainty. *He wants to find his kidnappers as much as I do, but they're freezing him out.*

Well, maybe her father needed a little normalcy after everything he'd been through. And if so, she'd help him get it. But in the meantime, she'd do a little digging of her own.

Gaia sat up straight and squared her shoulders. "Okay, I'm in," she said. "Actually, we can go tomorrow. We have the day off for some teacher's conference."

"Good. Tomorrow it is," her father said, squeezing both her shoulders from behind. "We'll go over to Seventh and hit the stores." He turned, hands in the pockets of his khakis, and looked around the living room. "It'll be a whole new start. Out with the old, in with the new."

Gaia smiled slightly and looked up at Jake, who was staring right at her. She felt a flutter in her heart as their eyes locked. Maybe Jake could help her with her investigation. She was clueless as to where to start, but maybe they could figure that out—together.

A whole new start, she thought. *Out with the old, in with the new.*

OLIVER SAT IN ONE OF THE FEW

Rejection chairs in his brownstone in Brooklyn, staring at the telephone on the table next to him. A half-empty bottle of scotch reflected the glow from the desk lamp that afforded the only light in the room. He took a swig from his glass and braced himself as the warm liquid burned down his throat.

It's just a phone call, he told himself. *You've taken phone calls from the President of the United States in your day. Just get it over with.*

He placed the tumbler down, picked up the receiver, and quickly punched in Gaia and Tom's number. He had no idea why he was overcome with such trepidation. Yes, there was a lot of bad history between him and his brother and niece, but that had all changed. They had fought side by side in Russia. They had escaped together. And even if he and Tom had been at each other's throats half the time, going through those experiences together had brought them closer. He could feel it. Tom must have been feeling it, too.

The phone rang a few times and he finally heard someone pick up at the other end. Oliver started to smile.

"Tom Moore," his brother said stiffly.

"Hello, Tom. How are you settling in?"

Silence. Oliver's heart thumped almost painfully.

"Tom?"

"I don't want you calling here again," his brother said, his tone impossibly cold.

"Tom, please. I just thought you and Gaia and I could get together," Oliver said, sitting forward in his seat. "To talk things over. . . maybe have a meal—"

"Until I know with absolute certainty that you had nothing to do with my kidnapping and with the threats to Gaia's life, I have nothing to say to you. And I don't want you contacting her," Tom said. "Do you understand?"

Oliver struggled for words—a unique experience for him. Usually he could be smooth under any circumstance, could sweet-talk anyone and everyone he came into contact with. It was all part of his CIA training. But this. . . this flat-out rejection from his only brother—his twin—was too much, even for him.

"Tom, I—"

"Stay away from my daughter, Oliver. Don't test me on this."

And with that, the line went dead. Oliver held the receiver against his face, unable to move. He hadn't expected Tom to jump up and down and do cartwheels over the phone call, but this completely disrespectful treatment was uncalled for. After everything he'd done to bring Tom home safely, to help his brother and his daughter, he certainly didn't deserve *this*.

With his hand shaking, Oliver slowly lowered the receiver onto the cradle. He took a steadying breath and lifted his drink again, downing the rest of it in one quick gulp.

It's going to be okay, he told himself, bracing his forearm with his other hand to stop the shaking. To stop the hot blood coursing through his veins from pushing him toward the edge—toward anger. *He'll come around eventually.*

But his thoughts were cold comfort to him, alone in his dark, unfurnished home. What did he have to do to get back in Tom's good graces? How many times would he have to prove himself?

AS THE SUN BEGAN TO SET OVER THE

city, and its red-gold light reflected off the mirrored façade of the more modern buildings, Gaia walked toward the front desk at Wallace and Wenk, the law offices that doubled as a front for the CIA's underground New York headquarters. Per Jake's advice, she was

By the Rules

wearing the most responsible outfit she could piece together—her cleanest jeans topped by a light blue button-down shirt belonging to Jake that he hadn't worn since the ninth grade. Her hair was back in a bun, and she tried to walk with her chin up and her eyes straight ahead. The small, mousy woman behind the counter smiled tightly as Gaia approached.

"May I help you?" she asked.

"Yeah, I'm here to see Mr. Lawrence Vance," Gaia said, thrumming her fingers on the glossy marble countertop. The receptionist eyed her gnarled fingernails and Gaia clasped her hands behind her back.

"I see. And your name?" the woman asked dubiously.

"Gaia Moore. Please tell him I'm Tom Moore's daughter," Gaia said.

The receptionist hit a few buttons on the switchboard in front of her, then turned away from Gaia to speak into the receiver. This was never going to work—Gaia could feel it. It was Jake's idea to play by the rules—if she wanted to find out what was going on with Natasha and Tatiana, she would have to gain the respect and trust of the CIA. But Gaia didn't like it. She would have preferred to figure out a way to break in after dark and deal with things *her* way.

Of course, this was the CIA. Her way would probably get her shot dead on first sight.

"I'm to show you to one of our waiting rooms," the mousy woman said, seeming surprised as she hung up the phone. "Nancy, will you cover the phones for a sec?" she asked her counterpart. Then she led Gaia over to a bank of silver elevators at the back of the lobby. Once inside the sleek elevator, the woman stuck a key into a silver button, turned it, and depressed the button. The elevator moved swiftly down and Gaia almost lost her balance. She'd been expecting to be going up.

When the doors slid open again, a stern-looking woman, not much older than Gaia, stood in front of them in a gray suit and white blouse. She made an expression that may have passed for a smile in CIA circles.

"Ms. Moore. What a pleasure to meet you," she said, extending her hand. "I'm Agent Rosenberg."

Gaia shook the woman's hand and Agent Rosenberg looked at the receptionist. "You can go now, Jean. I'll take it from here."

"Later, Jean," Gaia said as the doors slid closed. Then she eyed Agent Rosenberg's skinny legs, her even skinnier arms, her sleek black hair. "You don't look like an agent," she said.

"Neither do you," Agent Rosenberg replied. "But I hear you can fight like one. Follow me."

Gaia did as she was told, keeping with the `play-by-the-rules plan`, but every cell in her body was jumping around: chaos. Natasha and Tatiana were here somewhere and it was all she could do to keep from laying the agent out and opening doors at random.

"In here, please," Agent Rosenberg said.

Gaia stepped inside a small office and Agent Rosenberg sat down at a silver table, looking up at Gaia expectantly. Gaia remained standing.

"Is Vance coming?" she asked.

"No. The director is otherwise occupied," Agent Rosenberg said. "What can I do for you?"

"They sent you to deal with me?" Gaia asked with a scoff. "You must be an intern or something like that."

"Actually I'm a special agent first class, and they wouldn't have sent me if they didn't want you to know that you're very important to this organization," Rosenberg said, her words clipped.

"But not important enough for the director," Gaia said.

"'Fraid not," Rosenberg replied, breaking diction temporarily. "Now, what can I do for you?"

Gaia stood across the room from Agent Rosenberg and crossed her arms over her chest.

"My dad was taken off the Petrova interrogation," Gaia said. "I want him back on."

"I'm sorry. We can't do that," Rosenberg said with a semblance of a smile.

"Then I want to interrogate them," Gaia said.

"I'm sorry. We can't do that," Rosenberg said.

"Why are you even bothering with me?" Gaia snapped.

"Why are you even bothering asking for things you know I can't give you?" Rosenberg replied, leaning forward. "You're a smart girl. Start asking the smart questions—the ones I might be able to help you with."

Gaia narrowed her focus, feeling as if she'd been reprimanded, but also feeling as if she'd been thrown a bone. She pulled over a metal chair and sat down, eyeing Agent Rosenberg, sizing her up.

"Can you tell me what they're saying in there?" Gaia asked finally.

"Not much," Agent Rosenberg replied.

"Have they given you any leads?" Gaia asked.

"Not yet," Agent Rosenberg said. But this time, there was a note of optimism in her tone. Gaia shifted in her seat.

"What's your plan to get them to talk?" she asked.

Agent Rosenberg smirked. "Now there's something I have been authorized to tell you. We've decided to split the prisoners up and offer them whichever bargaining chip would get them to talk. The only problem is, we're not entirely certain what that chip might be. We have a hunch, but we're not entirely certain."

There was a moment of silence as Gaia took this in. Agent Rosenberg gazed right into her eyes as if it were as easy as staring at a TV. Gaia felt a sudden moment of affinity with the woman. She seemed as close to fearless as any other human Gaia had come in contact with. She was all about control.

"You want my help," Gaia said.

Agent Rosenberg nodded. "Perceptive girl."

"What do I get?" Gaia asked.

"You get to help us find the person or persons who kidnapped your father," Rosenberg replied coolly. "And I will also keep you informed, as much as security clearance allows."

Gaia took a deep breath. It was better than nothing. "Okay, fine," she said. "Tell Tatiana that if she talks you'll let Natasha go and tell Natasha that if she talks you'll let Tatiana go."

"Interesting," Rosenberg said, nodding. "Offer the other prisoner's freedom, not her own."

"Trust me," Gaia said, feeling fairly satisfied with herself. "That's the only way to get to those two."

You know you're in trouble when leaving messages becomes as addictive as playing video games. You're sitting in your room, and you know you shouldn't start, say, Super Collapse up again. Your eyes are dry and your fingers are twitching and you're definitely feeling the early onset of carpal tunnel syndrome, but you can't help yourself. You keep thinking, *This is it. This is the time I'm going to get to the next level or beat my high score.* And so you click it open again, and you play, and you almost never beat that high score because now it's two A.M. and you're dehydrated and dizzy and you no longer know what the point of the game is anyway.

But the whole leaving messages thing is even worse. Because if you play that video game until two o'clock in the morning, the only one that's going to know about it is you. And even though you have a headache the next morning and you can see the little Collapse boxes stacking up in your head when you close your eyes, your shame is all your own. There are no witnesses. And you can live with your own shame. You can delete the damn game from your hard drive and move on.

But the messages are a different story because every time you pick up the phone and dial, you know somewhere in the back of your mind that someone else is going to hear whatever rambling idiocy you're about to spew. You know they're going to hear all two, three, five, ten messages and you know that no matter what you say, all that's going to register is, *"Hi, I'm a psycho and I can't control myself."* And yet you think you can fix it. You think you can say just the right thing to make all those other messages disappear.

You're delusional. And this time, you have witnesses.

Seeing
Oliver, she
was glad
she'd come.
Her uncle
looked
like
something
out of a
Charles
Dickens novel.

the hermit

"YOU SHOULDN'T BE HERE," OLIVER said the second he opened the door for Gaia on Saturday morning. His face was covered with patchy stubble and he looked as if he hadn't slept for more than five minutes the night before. His tired eyes were full of bitterness and sorrow.

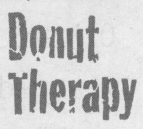

Donut Therapy

"What's wrong?" Gaia asked, clutching her bag full of donuts and coffee.

Oliver didn't answer. He turned and walked back into the house, leaving the door only slightly ajar. To follow or not to follow, that was the question.

Gaia used the toe of her Doc Marten to push the door open and stepped out of the sunlight and into the dark depths of the brownstone. Oliver had kept the curtains drawn the whole time they were hiding out here, searching for clues on the whereabouts of her father, and it seemed her uncle hadn't let the sun in once since then. Didn't he know they were out of danger? Or had he just gotten used to the darkness?

"Gaia, I don't want to get you into trouble with your father," Oliver said wearily, lowering himself into a creaking chair at the one small, chipped table that stood against the far wall. There was a legal pad in front of him with a long list down the right side. Oliver capped the pen he'd obviously been using and pushed both things aside.

"If he knew you were here he would not be happy," he added.

Pretty depressing. *It looks like my donut therapy idea was long overdue,* Gaia thought. She'd woken up that morning and realized that Oliver might be hurting for company since Jake had left. She'd been up and out the door before her father had even stirred from his bedroom and now, seeing Oliver, she was glad she'd come. Her uncle looked like something out of a Charles Dickens novel.

"Tell me something I don't know," Gaia said with a smirk. "In case you hadn't noticed, I tend not to listen to authority."

Oliver smirked and nodded slowly as if he were sharing a private joke with himself.

Gaia placed the large waxed paper bag down on the table and started to unload the goods—a box of six fresh donuts and two huge cups of steaming coffee. She sat down across from Oliver and pulled her coffee over to her, popped the tab back, and inhaled the comforting scent. Oliver slid his own cup over the table and wrapped both hands around it. She noticed that his skin was dry to the point of cracking and that his fingers looked very pale.

Gaia swallowed hard and tried not to stare. After the mission in Russia she'd hoped that Oliver would start to come out of his shell a bit—start coming out of the brownstone every once in a while—but clearly he didn't feel he was ready for that yet. He was slowly turning into a hermit.

Maybe if Dad hadn't made him feel like the enemy, Gaia thought bitterly. *Maybe if he'd felt the least bit of warmth from his brother, he'd be feeling better about life.*

"Have you thought about. . . I don't know. . . getting some new furniture? A couple of lamps, maybe?" Gaia asked, looking around the depressing room. She was supposed to go shopping with her father that afternoon and wondered if she could sneak in a couple of purchases for her uncle. The man was going to go Unabomber if he didn't get a little light in this place. Maybe a painting or a poster to brighten things up.

Oliver's brows came together over his nose. "Hadn't really considered it."

Gaia's heart thumped. "Why not?" she asked. "I mean, you are going to stay here, right?" The last thing she wanted was for Oliver to skip town. Not now. Not before he made up with her father. She knew it was optimistic and probably very stupid of her, but she had this picture somewhere in the back of her mind— a picture of her and what was left of her family sitting down to dinner together, laughing and talking and just. . . being normal.

"I don't know, Gaia," Oliver said, his features softening a bit. "I think it might be better if I just. . . if I just disappeared."

"Why? Because that's what my father wants?" Gaia

asked, reddening. Oliver looked as if he'd been slapped. "I mean, because that's what you *think* my father wants?" she added. "He's just being him. He's just being. . . careful. He's going to come around eventually."

Oliver took a deep breath and leaned back. "I hope you're right," Oliver said. He placed his coffee cup down and slid the legal pad over so that it was resting in front of him again. He squinted down at the page, concentrating.

"What is that?" Gaia asked, grabbing a chocolate-covered donut and chomping into it. She used the back of her hand to wipe the crumbs from her mouth and leaned over to see the list as Oliver turned it toward her.

It was a list of names. And Sam Moon's was at the top.

"Okay," Gaia said, gazing at Oliver. "I still don't know what it is."

Oliver smiled slightly—sadly. "It's a list of people I need to make amends with," he explained. "I just started it, but I have a feeling it's going to get much, much longer."

Gaia looked down at the thirty or so names, her heart constricting. Oliver really was trying. He was trying so hard. And he was living out here by himself in Brooklyn like some kind of criminal banished from society. Why couldn't her father see how much he had changed?

Because he killed your mother. Because he tried to kill you on numerous occasions. Because he's evil, a little voice in Gaia's head told her.

But he wasn't evil. Not anymore. He was Oliver now, not Loki. And sooner or later her father was going to have to recognize that.

"Do you think Sam would talk to me?" Oliver asked, his eyebrows rising.

That question caught her completely off guard. She choked on her donut. "I don't know," Gaia replied truthfully. It was going to be a hard sell. Sam had lost several months of his life thanks to Loki. "But I'll see what I can do."

"That's all I can ask," Oliver replied, picking the list up again with two hands—almost reverently. When he looked up at Gaia once more, she could tell he was having one of his emotional moments. She concentrated to keep herself from squirming. She hated this part.

"Thank you for coming here, Gaia," Oliver said softly, his eyes moist around the edges. "It means a lot that you're still here for me."

"I know," Gaia said awkwardly. She reached up and pushed the bag of donuts toward him. "Eat something already."

Oliver smiled and picked up a jelly donut. Together they sat in companionable silence, until every last crumb was polished off.

TOM MOORE WALKED THROUGH THE

Decisions

Pottery Barn on 59th and Lexington, trying not to let his exhaustion and frustration show on his face. Like most men, he'd never been much of a shopper. He didn't have strong opinions about anything. Antique or modern, wood-finish or painted, steel or wrought iron. It was all the same to him. One would think that this blasé attitude would make this whole excursion easier—that he could pretty much just buy whatever he saw and be happy—but his lack of conviction just made him more irritated with himself.

He wanted to make a home with his daughter. And he hated that he didn't care what was in it. All he cared about was that it didn't look like it once belonged to Natasha.

"Dad? What about this bed?" Gaia asked from somewhere nearby.

Tom turned and saw Gaia standing next to a large, heavy, wooden bed with a high headboard. He was struck for the millionth time by how very much she looked like Katia—more and more each day. He smiled slightly, remembering how adorably frustrated his wife used to get whenever she took him out to the shops.

"Just make a decision, Tom!" she would say, clutching two bedsheets in her delicate hands. "Plain white or blue stripes? Have an opinion!"

"I like it," Tom said, walking over to Gaia and running his hand along the carvings at the top of the headboard. "This is the one."

Gaia smiled, clearly relieved that he'd finally picked something out. After five stores in all corners of the city, she had to be getting a bit tired. And while Gaia had quickly selected a new bed, desk, and linens at some of the independently owned stores downtown, the only thing Tom had so far was a lamp to replace the one he'd thrown at the wall in a fit of rage the day before. The truth was, the bed didn't inspire any great feelings within Tom, but the memory of Katia had. And he figured he might as well make this trip easier on their daughter like he was never able to for his wife.

Gaia walked over to a wall of shelves that held packages of sheets and pillowcases in brushed, brown silk.

"These look like they're you," Gaia said. "I mean, as much as sheets can *be* a person."

Tom smiled. "How so?"

Gaia considered, obviously choosing her words. She never would have admitted it, but Tom knew she was enjoying this shopping spree.

"They're manly man sheets," she said finally, blushing slightly. "Sophisticated, but—"

Tom reached out and ran his fingers over the smooth, velvety silk. "Sophisticated, but soft and mushy like your old man?" he joked, as he patted his less than solid stomach.

"Exactly," Gaia said with a laugh.

"Okay, so I'm a little more doughy than-usual. . . . Next time I go to a Siberian prison, I'll have to remember my free weights." This made Gaia laugh even harder. Tom loved entertaining his daughter in this way.

Tom sat down on the bed and leaned back into the faux fur pillows, watching her as she searched for the right size. He took a deep breath and tried to calm the nerves that seemed to rear up every few minutes.

This was insane. He should be at headquarters right now, grilling Natasha. Deciphering what her cryptic clues about the past were all about. He should be trying to find out everything he could about his brother and the role he'd had in Tom's kidnapping. Instead he was kicking back in a superstore with fake fur bristles tickling the back of his neck.

"So, I went to see Oliver this morning," Gaia said suddenly, her back to him.

"What?" Tom blurted, bolting up. He felt all the blood rush to his head. "Gaia—"

"Dad, I think you should hear him out," Gaia said, tossing a set of sheets on the bed next to his bent leg.

"I am *not* going to hear him out and you are not going over there again!" Tom shouted, standing.

He looked at his daughter and his heart sank. She

suddenly seemed about four years old, standing there looking up at him with those wide, confused eyes. Tom glanced around the store and saw that a pair of older women and a younger couple had all frozen in place and were gaping at him. Tom felt his skin prickle with the heat of embarrassment.

"I'm sorry," he said quietly, coming around the bed. He ran his hand over Gaia's shoulder and down her arm, then squeezed her hand. "Gaia, I'm sorry," he repeated. "I'm just on edge. And when it comes to my brother. . ."

"I. . . I know," Gaia said, clearing her throat. "You don't have to explain." She moved away from him and made a big show of inspecting a set of old-fashioned clocks on a shelf at eye-level. Tom felt his chest empty out the moment she stepped away.

"But I do," Tom said, standing next to her. "For some reason I just haven't been able to control my emotions since we've been back," he told her. "But I'm working on it. I *am* sorry, Gaia."

"I know," Gaia said again. But this time she turned and looked him in the eye, attempting a smile.

"Listen, I know you care for your uncle, but I want you to trust me on this one," he told her. "I don't want you seeing him again until we know for sure that he had nothing to do with Natasha and Tatiana's attempts on your life. I don't trust him yet, Gaia. Just. . . humor me."

Gaia looked up into his eyes, her own wide and sure. "Okay, Dad," she said. "I won't see him again."

She was lying. She might not have even known it, but she was. Tom knew that Gaia would see Oliver again if she wanted to. She was an independent girl— always had been. And Tom had always admired it. Unfortunately it had also always scared him. Independence and fearlessness were not a good combination.

But as he looked into her eyes, he decided not to press the issue. Gaia had survived this long, mostly on her own. She was an intelligent, instinctive person, and Tom was proud of her. He was going to have to trust her to do what was right. Even if it meant swallowing his pride and keeping his mouth shut.

"Thank you," Tom replied. "Believe me, I want you to be right about this. You have no idea how much I want you to be right."

"I know," Gaia said, looking away. She lifted her hand toward the bed and let it slap down against her leg again. "So, you want to start loading up on this stuff so we can get out of here? I want to get home and see if they delivered *my* new stuff yet."

"Definitely," Tom said, feeling his head clear. "But I don't want any of that fur stuff," he added, finally making a real decision. "Not my style."

"I had a feeling," Gaia said with a smile.

She grabbed a basket and started to pick sheets and

shams and pillowcases off the shelf. Tom smiled wistfully as he watched her work. He promised himself there would be no more thinking about work and no more talking about Oliver for the rest of the day. All he wanted was to have a nice time with his daughter.

SAM STOOD OUTSIDE THE DOOR TO

The Gaia Loop

Gaia's apartment and squared his shoulders. He tried to ready himself for whatever response she might give him. He had no idea what she was thinking after hearing all his messages—mainly because she'd never bothered to return them—but he had to find out. He had to know, once and for all, if what they had between them could still be salvaged.

The door swung open and Sam's heart skipped a few dozen beats. Gaia's face was flushed and her eyes were sparkling with something that could only be called happiness. Her hair was sticking out wildly around her face, having fallen loose from the ponytail that still held some of it back. She was wearing a white T-shirt and a pair of baggy jeans. When she reached up to smooth some hair behind her ear, the T-shirt rode up and exposed a tiny strip of her flat stomach.

"Sam," she said, the flush deepening. She crossed her arms over her chest and held herself. "Hi."

"Hey," Sam said. What was he supposed to say next? *Just wanted to see why you didn't return my calls.* Lame. He really should have thought this through.

"Gaia! Who is it?" a voice called from back in the living room. A man's voice.

Sam looked past Gaia into the apartment, where he could see basically nothing. "Bad timing?" he asked, his heart slamming into his rib cage.

"No!" Gaia said, finally stepping back. "Come in."

Sam followed Gaia past the kitchen and into the living room, which was littered with huge broken-down cardboard boxes, random pieces of oddly shaped Styrofoam, and enough bubble wrap to keep his fingers popping for days. Sam's eyes lit up when he saw Gaia's father stand up from behind a desk he was apparently assembling. At least, he hoped it was her father. The other option would have sent him running for the door.

"Sam Moon!" the man said brightly. He wiped his palm on the back of his jeans and held his hand out. "It's good to see you again."

"Mr. Moore," Sam said, shaking hands with the man. His grip was strong and his hands were calloused. "You're back."

"Thanks to Gaia," Mr. Moore said, smiling at his

49

daughter before returning to the manufacturer's directions he had laid out on the floor.

Sam turned to Gaia, a million questions in his mind. Last he heard, Gaia's father had disappeared from the hospital and she had no idea who had taken him or where, let alone why. Now the man was miraculously back home and building furniture in the living room like nothing had ever happened. A person could definitely miss *a lot* when they were out of the Gaia loop for a few short weeks.

A cold, hard ball formed around Sam's heart and he realized he was hurt. Hurt over being frozen out of Gaia's life. But he made himself remember that she *had* tried to apologize and it was he who pushed her away. He'd caused this.

"Oh, we just bought some new stuff," Gaia said, either misreading the question in his eyes or deciding to answer the easiest one first. "We're. . . redecorating."

"Cool," Sam said for lack of something better to say.

"So, what are you doing here?" Gaia asked, ever blunt.

"I. . . uh. . . was just hoping we could talk," Sam said quietly, moving toward the dining room table and away from her father. His shoved his hands into the pockets of his suede jacket and curled them into fists.

Gaia glanced in her dad's direction and Sam did the same. Clearly she sensed this was a conversation that couldn't take place with a parent around.

"Dad, I'm going to take a break," Gaia said, picking her jacket up off one of the dining room chairs. "I'll be back in a little while."

"Don't worry about me," her father said, his hand appearing from behind the back of the desk. "I'm sure I'll still be right here when you get back."

Gaia slipped into her battered army jacket and led the way out to the hall and the elevator. Sam could feel the tension between them as they stood side by side, watching the numbers light up as they descended to the lobby. He wished that he knew what she was thinking. He wished that he had a better handle on what *he* was thinking. All he knew was that his heart was racing and that he wanted this to go well.

The only question was: What did "well" mean? Did it mean that they would come out of this day as friends? Did it mean that they would come out of this day as a couple? Somewhere deep inside he knew that he wanted the latter, but would probably settle for the former.

His life was a lot less interesting without Gaia around—a lot less passionate and exciting and, yeah, dangerous, but still. . . . The occasional danger was a small price to pay for the other stuff.

Sam wanted back in the Gaia loop. He just hoped she was willing to let him in.

51

GAIA SAT DOWN ACROSS FROM SAM

at a back table at the Mikonos diner, wondering what the hell to say to break the excruciating silence. She wanted to apologize for not returning his calls. She wanted to ask him what had prompted them after he basically told her he never wanted to see her again. She wanted to know what he was thinking as he picked up the menu and pretended to look it over.

But every time she tried to formulate one of those questions in her mind it either came out sounding desperate, pathetic, or accusatory, none of which she actually felt.

"Oh, hey, Dmitri's back," Sam said, cutting into her thoughts. "He told me to tell you."

"Done laying low?" Gaia asked. "That's cool. I talked to him a couple of times on his cell, but I had no idea where he was."

"Yeah. He didn't even tell me," Sam said.

They fell back into awkward silence, each gazing out the window. Gaia was psyched by this new development. If Dmitri was back in town maybe he could help her track down her father's kidnapper. He had resources, contacts at the CIA. Between him and Rosenberg, maybe she could get somewhere.

She sighed and looked at the cow-spotted clock above the counter. If someone didn't say something soon she was going to have to bail. Of course, there was *one* thing she *had* to talk to Sam about and now was as good a time as any. Gaia took a sip from the water glass that the busboy had slapped down on the table and cut right to the chase.

"My uncle wants to meet with you," she said.

Sam dropped the menu down flat on the table. "You're kidding me."

"No. I know it's a lot to ask, but—"

"A lot to ask? Gaia, the guy kept me in an eight-by-eight cell for six months! Why the hell would I want to meet with him?" Sam blurted.

"But it wasn't him," Gaia told him. "You know that. He only wants to meet with you because he wants to apologize for what Loki did."

Sam lifted his hand and rubbed at his forehead with his thumb and forefinger. He pressed his eyes closed and took a steadying breath. "I don't want to talk about this right now," he said finally.

Gaia heard the pain in his voice and the effort Sam was making to control it. She decided to drop the subject—for now. She'd broached it and now he could have some time to think it over.

"Fine," she said as the waitress approached. Gaia ordered a Coke and a plate of cheese fries, and Sam asked for a black coffee.

"So. . . ," he said as the waitress scurried away.

"So," she replied. She was going to let him bring it up, whatever it was. He was the one who had called her. He was the one who had come over. She wasn't going to say a word until he told her what he was thinking. It was a convenient decision to make since she had no idea what to think herself.

"So, your dad's back," Sam said, pushing his water glass back and forth between his hands. "That's amazing."

Gaia blinked. "Yeah. My uncle and I tracked him down, actually," she said. Instantly her thoughts turned to Jake and his role in rescuing her father. Should she tell Sam about him? And if so, what should she tell? The whole Jake thing was so complicated in her mind, she wasn't sure she could explain it to herself, let alone to Sam.

She also knew that whatever Sam was thinking, there was a chance he might shut down if she mentioned another guy. Even if she and Sam were no longer together, she knew that he would assume that she and Jake were more than friends if he knew what Jake had done for her. And if he thought they were more than friends, uncomfortableness would ensue. That was the last thing Gaia wanted.

"Where was he?" Sam asked, leaning back as the waitress placed their orders in front of them. "I mean, unless it's top secret."

"He was in Russia," Gaia replied. "We're still not sure who took him."

She shoved a few fries in her mouth and they

settled in her stomach like sticks. *We're still not sure who took him,* the words repeated in her mind. Maybe she shouldn't have left her father alone.

"Hey, it's okay," Sam said suddenly, reading her expression. "He's home now. You guys are going to be okay."

Gaia watched as Sam's hand slowly came down on top of her own. The warmth of his skin sent a shiver up her arm and she didn't pull away. It was amazing how comforting one touch could be. She had thought Sam was never going to touch her again.

"I know," she said.

His fingers closed a little more tightly around her palm and Gaia felt a jolt of something—something unpleasant. Something that felt a whole lot like guilt.

Jake, she thought, her stomach churning. *I feel guilty because of Jake.*

She swallowed hard and stared at Sam's hand on her own. This was a new and unexpected twist. She knew that she was attracted to Jake. She knew that he had pretty much become her best friend. But guilt over holding hands with another guy? How had it come to this?

You have to tell Sam, Gaia's inner voice told her. *Pull your hand away. Tell him it's over.*

But she couldn't. Sam held a huge part of Gaia's heart and he was finally here. He clearly cared about her and wanted to be part of her life. If she said anything now, that would all be obliterated. She wasn't ready to let go of him yet.

"What're you thinking?" Sam asked.

Tell him about Jake! Say something!

"Nothing," Gaia replied, removing her hand and picking up another fry. "I wasn't thinking about anything."

As she shoveled a few cheesy fries into her mouth, she decided that, for now, Jake was going to remain on the back burner. For now, she just wanted to be with Sam. She owed it to him, and to herself, to see if they could be friends again.

She could deal with her intense emotional confusion later.

I'm no good at this stuff. Never have been. Probably never will be. I suck at figuring out how people feel about me. But I suck even more at figuring out how I feel about them. It took me forever to figure out that the nausea I always felt around Sam was attraction. It took me even longer to realize that I was in love with Ed. But in both those cases, there were a million other factors to complicate things. There was Heather, for example. And there was the fact that being with anyone put that person in immediate danger. Sam was kidnapped because of me. Ed was almost killed. It made it kind of hard to even think about being close to someone.

But now. . . now things have changed. It's really as simple as that when you get down to it. There's nothing to protect Jake from. And even if there was, he's not a person who would tolerate being protected. He's made that

more than clear. So now I have to
deal. I have to deal with the
fact that, yeah, I'm attracted to
him. There, I said it. I have to
deal with the fact that when I
was with Sam today, I couldn't
stop thinking about Jake. I have
to deal with the fact that I look
forward to seeing him. That when
I'm with him my thoughts are
mostly positive. That whenever we
happen to touch or brush up
against each other, I get that
shiver all over my skin.

I have to deal. I have to figure out how I feel. Because there
aren't any more excuses not to.

To: X22
From: Y
Subject: RE: Prisoner 352, Codename Abel

   Receipt of message confirmed. Send all NYC
units into the field. I want daily reports on the
movements of Genesis, Cain, and Abel. Don't fail
me on this.

Could she really do this? Could she really just take off on the spur of the moment and go have fun?

time to try

"GAIA! WHAT A PLEASANT SURPRISE!"

Touched

Dmitri held the door to his Murray Hill apartment open for Gaia on Saturday morning and she smiled as she walked by. She may have been there on business, but she had a soft place in her heart for the kindly old man who had helped her bring Natasha to justice. It was good to see him again.

"How have you been?" Dmitri asked, settling into a cushy leather chair in his plush living room. Gaia sat across from him on the couch and leaned forward.

"Okay," she said. "But I need your help."

"What is it?" Dmitri asked, his expression growing concerned.

"The CIA put my father on forced leave and they won't let either one of us near Natasha and Tatiana," Gaia said in a rush. "Which means we're nowhere on the investigation into my father's kidnapping."

Dmitri nodded slowly, taking this in. "Why did they put your father on leave?"

"I don't know," Gaia said, standing up and starting to pace. "He won't tell me and neither will they."

"You talked to someone at the CIA?" Dmitri asked, raising his eyebrows. He brought his fingertips together under his nose in a contemplative pose as he watched her circle in front of him.

"Yeah, some special agent," Gaia said. "She's going

61

to grill Natasha and Tatiana separately. I told her what to dangle in front of them to make them talk, but who knows if it'll work. . . ."

Dmitri shifted in his seat and brought his hands together under his nose. "What did you tell her to do?"

Gaia really looked at him for the first time since the conversation started. There was a new tension in his voice. He was legitimately apprehensive. Gaia was touched.

"I told her to offer Natasha Tatiana's freedom and vice versa," she said with a shrug.

Dmitri narrowed his eyes and nodded, then took a deep breath. "Yes. Very wise," he said, now gazing off across the room. "That just might do the trick."

"Anyway, do you think there's anything you can do?" Gaia asked, sitting down on the edge of the couch again. "Can you call your guy at the CIA and see what he knows? Or. . . I don't know, use some of your other con-tacts—find out if they've gotten any rumblings out of Russia? Maybe people are talking about the rescue. . . ."

Dmitri sat in silence for a moment, eyeing her, mulling over everything she'd told him. Finally he sat up and leaned forward, resting his forearms on his knees. His face moved into the shaft of light coming from a nearby lamp, illuminating every last line and wrinkle in his weathered face.

"Gaia, I know you're not going to like this, but I think it's time for you to let this go," he said.

Gaia felt as if he'd just punched her right in the gut. With brass knuckles. "What? Let what go? The fact that Natasha and Tatiana betrayed us? The fact that someone kidnapped my father? What if they try it again?"

"They won't try it again," Dmitri said, his blue eyes sure. "Trust me."

"How can you know that?" Gaia demanded.

"You've already proven that you won't be intimidated—that you won't respond to their tactics," Dmitri said. "Believe me, Gaia. I know how these people work."

Gaia couldn't comprehend what she was hearing. She had been so sure that Dmitri would help her. So confident that he was her best ally in this. Why was he turning her down?

"Please, Gaia. It's time to move on," Dmitri said, reaching for her hands. "Let it go and live your life. Let the CIA do its job."

Gaia scoffed and stood again, pulling her hands from his. "You sound just like my father."

Dmitri chuckled and looked up at her. "I suppose I should take that as a compliment."

"Whatever," Gaia said, turning her back on him and heading for the door.

"Gaia! I want you to know that whatever happens, I will always be here for you!" Dmitri called after her.

Gaia paused for only a second, then kept walking,

wondering why she had hesitated at all. Why those words had for some reason touched a chord within her heart.

"Yeah," she said under her breath. "Thanks for nothing."

TOM WALKED TOWARD CENTRAL PARK,

his arms crossed over his chest, his eyes trained on the ground. He took a few long, deep breaths of the fresh spring air and felt the soothing warmth of the sun wash over him. Once he'd finished putting together Gaia's new furniture that morning, he'd found himself slowly going stir-crazy. His new bed and dresser were going to be delivered later in the week and he still couldn't seem to make himself comfortable among Natasha's things. He felt more stifled in that apartment with her books and her knickknacks and her scent than he had in any prison cell he'd ever had to call home.

Who was she working for? Tom wondered for the ten billionth time since he'd learned that Natasha was, in fact, the enemy. *She had to be working for someone. Who was it? The Russian Mafia? The Russian Secret Service? One of the newer spy organizations?*

He entered the park and passed by a few empty benches, not ready to sit yet. He had too much pent-up energy to expend. He'd walk the whole way to the other side and back if he had to. Whatever it took for him to figure this out.

Of course, the problem was, he was fairly certain he already had it figured out. As much as Gaia wanted to believe otherwise, Tom knew that Loki had to have been the one pulling the strings. It was the only scenario that made sense. No one had questioned him while he was in Russia. No one had tortured him or demanded he divulge his secrets. There didn't seem to be any point to him being there other than to keep him from being here. Who would go to all those lengths to remove him from his daughter other than Loki?

"Damn it," Tom said through his teeth. He stuffed his hands under his arms and clamped his elbows down, coiling in on himself. *How had Loki done it?* That was what he wanted to know. *How had he faked a coma? How had he given orders from a hospital room? How had he convinced Gaia that he was Oliver again?*

I need to talk to Natasha. She's the only one who knows, Tom thought, trying not to notice the mother who was pulling her toddler to her as he passed by, clearly disturbed by his whacked-out demeanor. *How could I have been so stupid? How could I have let her get to me?*

The answer, he knew, was simple. He let her get to him because he was in love with her. And her betrayal stung more than anything he'd suffered in the past. She'd fooled him into opening a heart that had been closed for a decade, and then she'd turned on him. If he was ever going to figure out what was going on with her and her daughter and Loki, he was going to have to get past that.

Tom paused at a fork in the paved pathway. He forced himself to uncurl his arms. Forced himself to look up at the oncoming dusk. He breathed in and out, expanding his chest and closing his eyes. He breathed in and out and `told himself to let go`. He had to. For his daughter. For his own sanity.

When he opened his eyes again, he looked at the two paths that lay ahead. One wound up and into the budding bushes and trees, the other was straight and sloped down toward the center of the park. Tom turned right and took the easier path. He wanted to stroll. He wanted to relax. It was `time to let go`.

He'd only taken a few long strides when the trill of his cell phone surprised him. He pulled it out of his pocket and flipped it open in one smooth motion.

"Moore here," he said into the mouthpiece.

"Agent Moore, it's Director Vance. There's been a development."

Tom blinked and stepped off the pathway to let a pair of skateboarders pass. "What kind of development?" he asked, his pulse beginning to race.

"We need you to come in," the deep, throaty voice replied. "Now."

"What about taking some time off?" Tom said, unabashedly enjoying this. They needed him. He knew they needed him.

"I'm ending it," Vance replied firmly. "I expect to see you in fifteen."

GAIA SAT ON THE COUCH ON SATURDAY

Used Undies

evening, brooding over her meeting with Dmitri. For the last hour she'd been alternating between obsessive irritation and obsessive brainstorming—trying to think of other ways to help her dad. He'd left her a message saying he was going back to work, which was good, but that didn't mean they were putting him back on the case. He might still need her, and even if he didn't, there was no way to stop her mind from obsessing.

When the doorbell rang, however, her thoughts came to a screeching stop. She jumped up, crossed the living room, and slipped the cover on the peephole aside.

Jake, she thought, her heart responding with the usual thump, much to her chagrin.

"I know you're there. I heard the peephole thing move," Jake said.

Gaia rolled her eyes and opened the door. Jake looked even more perfect in full, undistorted size than he had through the peephole. He was wearing black pants and shoes and a formfitting burgundy T-shirt that made his olive skin look even darker. His black leather jacket was new—at least she hadn't seen it before—and his hair was slightly gelled.

"Why are you dressed like that?" Gaia asked, stepping aside so that he could come in.

"It's Saturday night," Jake replied, opening his hands. "I think the more appropriate question is why are *you* dressed like *that?*"

Gaia flushed and crossed her arms over her chest. After she had returned from Dmitri's that afternoon, she'd taken a shower and braided her still-wet hair down her back. Then she'd slipped into her most comfortable cargo pants, a black T-shirt, and a black hooded sweatshirt for her night on the couch. What did Jake expect her to do, lounge around in silk and cashmere?

"So, you came here to insult my wardrobe?" Gaia asked.

"You started it," Jake said. He clapped his hands together and grinned. "Actually, I came here to take you out. Whatever you want to do, wherever you want to go."

Gaia blinked and drew herself up straight. Wait. Had he just asked her out? Where was the awkwardness? The agonizing silence? How was she supposed to have the time to get all mortified and embarrassed and confused if he just sprung it on her like that?

"I. . . uh. . ."

Okay, there it was. `Total loss of communication skills.` This felt more familiar.

"Come on, what do you do for fun?" Jake asked, his high energy bursting out of him and ricocheting off the walls. Gaia had a mental vision of herself ducking and dodging to avoid being hit by a shot of Jake oomph.

"What do I do for fun. . . ?" Gaia repeated, stalling.

This is pathetic, she thought, racking her brain. *I don't have an answer to that question.* But when had she ever had the chance to think about it? When had she ever been misery-free long enough to even consider having fun? Yeah, she'd had a few laughs with Ed, but she couldn't exactly tell Jake that she hung out with Ed for fun. Besides, hanging out with him was not an option. Not anymore.

"Um. . . chess?" Gaia said finally, pathetically.

Jake, understandably, laughed. "You have to be kidding me," he said, walking over and standing across from her. "You live in one of the most kickass cities in the world. There are a million things to do here and you pick chess."

"It's. . . challenging," Gaia said, defeated. She let her shoulders slump and looked up into his eyes. She felt like the biggest geek in the world, standing in front of some popular, fun-loving guru and begging him to help her become functional in society.

"Okay, you need help," Jake said, as if reading her mind.

He abruptly turned left and walked down the hall toward her bedroom. Gaia followed, somehow resisting the urge to tackle him to the floor before he got there. Her room was a constant mess, with tangles of clothes, cupcake wrappers, soda cans, and who knew what else littering the floor. If he went in there, he was sure to get a glimpse of something embarrassing, like socks with holes in them or bras with fraying straps or worst of all, used undies.

Please don't let him see any used underwear, Gaia thought, squeezing her eyes shut as she entered the room.

But Jake didn't even look around. He went straight to her closet and pulled out a slim-fitting black turtleneck. He tossed it at her and then started going through a pile of jeans—Tatiana's jeans.

"I'm *not* wearing her clothes," Gaia said. She grabbed a pair of white cotton panties off the floor and stuffed it under her new pillows.

"Understood," Jake replied, turning to her side of the closet again. "Do you own anything that isn't army green?"

Gaia flushed. Why had he come over here? To remind her of how unappealing she was? To show her that she didn't even own one single piece of clothing that a guy would find attractive? Jake was turning out to have some serious nerve.

"You know. . . ," Gaia began, but she never got to finish. Jake gave up on the closet and stepped so close to Gaia her nose was practically pressed into his chest. He reached around behind her and she felt a tug at the bottom of her braid. She held her breath as she felt his fingers running through her hair, fanning it out over her shoulders.

Jake pulled back and looked down at her, smiling almost gently. "Wear whatever you want," he said. "But I am taking you out of here."

Then he turned and walked out of the room, closing the door behind him. Still struggling to breathe, Gaia stepped in front of the full-length mirror that Tatiana had secured to the back of their door. Her hair was dry now and the haphazard braid had woven it in hundreds of loose waves. Gaia ran her fingers through it, trying to see whatever it was that had made Jake smile like that. She pulled it all over one shoulder and turned to the side.

Street rat, she thought.

"You coming?" Jake called out.

And right in front of her own reflection, Gaia smiled. Instantly. Purely. Without thinking about it. It was so odd, this actual spontaneous emotion. Could she really do this? Could she really just take off on the spur of the moment, forgo a night of obsessing and just have fun?

As she stood there, staring at herself, Gaia realized that she wanted to try.

She ripped off her sweatshirt and tee, pulled on the turtleneck, and yanked her hair out of the collar. Then she grabbed her denim jacket and her messenger bag and strode out of her room.

It was time to see what this fun thing was all about.

Getting There

"THANKS, MAN. I OWE YOU ONE," Jake said, slapping hands with his friend Derek Simms at the entrance to section 79 at Madison Square Garden.

Derek worked as a security guard at the Garden and had just smuggled Jake and Gaia in through a back entrance. The Knicks were playing a crappy team, so there were empty seats all over the arena and Derek was giving them two of the best.

"Yeah, when are you going to get a job I can take advantage of?" Derek asked, laughing as he gripped Jake's hand.

"We'll see," Jake said. They slapped each other's backs and then Derek loped off to return to his post.

Jake looked around and found Gaia standing at the top of the stairs, watching the action on the court. Her hair looked so touchable with all those waves, its million shades of blond shifting every time she moved. He could still feel its softness under his fingertips.

Get a grip, man, Jake told himself, rolling his shoulders back. Gaia was definitely a closed book and he knew it was going to take a lot of patience before he got to touch that hair again. He should count himself lucky that she didn't knee him in the groin the first time.

"Pretty sick, huh?" he asked, stepping up next to Gaia. Even with an undercapacity crowd, the place seemed to be filled with screaming fans in blue and orange. The butter-colored boards of the court gleamed under the bright lights and the loudspeaker blared a cavalry horn recording, prompting everyone in the arena to shout, "Charge!"

"I've never been to a game here," Gaia said, her eyes trained on Allan Houston as he drove down the court.

"Never? Well then, you'll need to have the full experience," Jake said. "I'll meet you at the seats."

"Where are you going?" Gaia asked, her blue eyes wide.

"Trust me," Jake said with a grin.

He waited until Gaia had settled into one of the seats Derek had pointed out, then turned and jogged over to the nearest souvenir stand. He picked out a blue-and-orange Knicks visor, a white tank top with a small logo on the chest, two huge foam fingers, and a tan fisherman-style cap for himself. The girl behind the counter eyed him like he was a crazy person as she handed over the goods and took a major wad of his cash. Then Jake hit the food counter and bought a couple of hot dogs and sodas. Balancing everything in his arms on the way back down the stairs, Jake thanked God that he had an aisle seat. Anyone he had to walk over would have killed him.

"What is all that?" Gaia asked as everyone around them stood up and cheered a killer three-point shot.

Jake placed the food tray down on his empty seat and handed the tank top, the visor, and the foam finger to Gaia, one by one.

"I'm not putting this stuff on," Gaia said flatly.

"Live a little, G," Jake told her, pulling the fisherman's cap down over his own eyes. He knew he probably looked like a tool, but that was the point. Gaia was going to have fun tonight if it killed him. Even if he had to embarrass the hell out of himself to make it happen.

He slipped the other foam finger on over his hand and raised it in the air. "Go, Knicks!" he shouted, tipping his head back. The fans all around him let out a huge cheer.

Gaia laughed and shook her head, her eyes dancing. Jake's heart flipped over. She'd laughed. He wasn't sure if he'd ever seen that before. Suddenly Gaia cleared her throat and looked away, flushing as if she'd done something wrong. Was it possible that she had actually never laughed before? Okay, probably not. But she obviously didn't do it much.

"Just put the tank top on over your shirt," he told her.

"What is it with you and dressing me?" Gaia asked. "Do you miss your Barbie dolls?"

Jake tucked his chin and looked up at her past the brim of his hat. "Put it on or you don't get the hot dog."

Gaia sighed and tilted her head so she could see the foot-long waiting for her in the cardboard tray. He could tell she was caving.

"Fine," she said finally. She took off her jacket, pulled the shirt on over her turtleneck, then slipped her jacket back on. While she was still adjusting herself, Jake placed the visor on her head and put the foam finger in her lap. Gaia rolled her eyes up and looked at the visor, then shook her head again, trying not to smile. She yanked the foam finger on and looked at Jake expectantly.

"Hot dog," she said, holding out her free hand.

Jake finally sat down, lifting the tray onto his lap, and handed her the goods. Gaia consumed a third of the hot dog in one huge bite.

"I'm good now," she said, chewing. And she actually did look good. She looked comfortable. . . content. And ridiculously cute. She lifted her foam finger to shoulder level. "Go, Knicks," she said quietly.

Jake smiled and bit into his own hot dog. "You're getting there."

TOM STOOD IN ONE OF THE DEBRIEFing rooms at the CIA's New York headquarters, completely calm and composed. He'd changed into a clean, starched suit and a tie and made sure there was no stray stubble on his face, no hair out of place on his head. Whatever he'd been called in to do, he was going to do it. He was going to prove that he was back on his game.

The door opened noiselessly and Director Vance entered the room, followed by two other agents—a young woman Tom had met two days ago named Clarissa Rosenberg, who was a behavioral specialist, and Trey Frenz, an agent Tom had trained with as a neophyte whom he'd never much liked. Tom ignored the presence of the other two and trained his eyes on Vance.

"Agent Moore, we've cut your leave of absence short—"

"Very short," Tom couldn't resist saying. Vance ignored his joke.

"Because since you left on Thursday afternoon, the prisoners have refused to speak to anyone," Vance continued.

Tom blinked. "What does that have to do with me?"

"They've refused to speak to anyone. . . but *you*," Vance said, averting his gaze for a split second. Tom felt a twitch on his lips and forced it away. He was not going to smile. He was not going to rub his triumph in his director's face. Vance was not the type of man who would find it amusing.

"We even took your daughter's advice, Agent Moore, offering each the other's freedom, but they didn't bite," Agent Rosenberg said. "At least not until now."

"Wait a second—Gaia was here?" Tom asked, baffled.

"She didn't tell you?" Agent Rosenberg asked.

"No," Tom said, making a mental note to ask a few questions of Gaia later. Now was no time to dwell on daughterly missteps. "Which one of them gave in? Which one is ready to talk?"

"Natasha," Agent Rosenberg said. "Call it a motherly instinct."

"So you're going back in there," Vance said. "Agent Rosenberg will be monitoring the prisoners' behavior, looking for body language, expressions, anything to indicate subterfuge."

"I'm sure I can—"

"I just want a second eye," Vance said. "These women know how to beat a lie detector but no one has ever snowed Agent Rosenberg."

The woman smiled slightly at the compliment, then quickly rearranged her sharp features.

"He's right. Your reputation precedes you," Tom told her.

"Thank you, Agent Moore," she said, a slight blush working its way across her high cheekbones.

"Agent Frenz is here to keep an eye on you, when I'm not in the observation area, and make sure you don't screw up again," Vance continued. Frenz smirked and Tom didn't give him the satisfaction of noticing.

"Agent Moore, I don't think I have to remind you of how delicate a situation this is," Director Vance said, stepping so close to Tom he could smell what the man had eaten for dinner. "Do you think you're ready for this?"

"I am, sir," Tom said, filled with conviction.

He did an internal systems check and was relieved to find that he was telling the truth. His pulse was slow, his body temperature normal. He didn't feel in the least bit stressed or excited or angry. All he wanted was to get it done.

"In fact, I'm quite looking forward to hearing what the prisoner has to say. . . ."

I've dated girls with secrets before, but Gaia is a completely new kind of cagey. I thought after the whole Tatiana shoot-out, after playing Triple X in Russia, after fighting for our lives together with her crazy father and uncle, after telling me about her mother's death that there couldn't possibly be anything else she was keeping from me.

But there's more. I know it. There's something else. Something else big. Something that's keeping her from trusting me completely. I can tell in the way she's always darting her eyes around when I ask questions. And sometimes I feel like she's on the verge of saying something and then she stops herself. I mean, what is it? She's pretty much with me most of the time.

Could her family have even more deep dark dramas that she doesn't want to reveal? Is that even possible? Is it something about her mom, maybe—or the reason her dad and uncle, like, hate each other?

Is it secret worthy? Something more than your standard dysfunctional spy-family crap?

I've got to admit, it scares me just a little bit. I mean, what could be bigger than the fact that her family is full of spies and that she's constantly a target? If there's something bigger than *that*, it's got to be a little scary.

The thing is, it's not scary enough to keep me away. It's not scary enough to even make a dent in the attraction I feel toward her. I've never felt anything like this before. And it's not just that she's hot. I mean, she *is*, but it's not just that. It's something else. There's just something about her. Something that makes me think about her all the time and crave her when I'm not around her.

So whatever that secret is, it's not going to scare me away. And sooner or later, she's going to tell me what it is. Because, unless I am totally off base, I think she's starting to feel the same way about me.

What had made
her think that
she could get
away with one
normal, fun
night? **trapped**
Didn't she know
the fates were
working against
her here?

GAIA WAS IN SUGAR HEAVEN. SHE
had passed Dylan's Candy Bar a
hundred times since its grand
opening, but had never stopped
in, and now that she was there,
she felt as if she'd come home,
made peace with the universe.
This place was built for her.

Freelance Vigilante Work

"I can't believe you've never
been in here," Jake said, watching as Gaia selected a huge bag
of Gummi Bears to add to her basket. "You live less
than ten blocks away."

"I know. I have issues," Gaia said. But now that she'd
been inside, she knew she was definitely coming back.
Possibly on a daily basis. The two-story candy shop had
every sugar-fix item Gaia had ever loved plus dozens of
things she'd never even heard of. They had Wonka Bars,
M&M's in every color in a Crayola box, and an ice
cream counter with flavors only dreamed of in heaven.

Maybe I should get a job here, she thought, imagin-
ing the damage she could do with an employee dis-
count.

"So, I tell you we can go anywhere in the city and
you drag me all the way back up and across town to go
to a place, like, ten blocks from your house," Jake said,
gnawing on a piece of black licorice.

"You said it was my choice," Gaia pointed out.

"Just wanted to be sure we're clear," Jake said, smiling. He looked down at her overflowing basket and frowned. "You're going to be on a sugar high for the rest of the year."

"Pretty much," Gaia said.

She took one last pass by the novelty wall, grabbed another Spider-Man pop, and deposited her basket on the counter. As the girl started to ring up her purchases, Jake pulled out his wallet. Gaia grabbed his wrist and pushed it back down under the counter.

"I got it," she said, the words "sugar daddy" ironically popping into her head. Every time Jake paid for something—cotton candy at the Knicks game, the cab to get back uptown—she felt more and more like this was a date. And the more she felt like it was a date, the more self-conscious she became. Gaia and dates did not mix.

Besides, she couldn't be out on a *date* while her father was interrogating Natasha and Tatiana. She couldn't be out on a date while her dad's kidnapper was still out there somewhere. It was just wrong.

Better for her subconscious to think she was just hanging out, even if on some level she was hoping this was a date, and Jake seemed to be hoping that, too. Her subconscious, after all, was the entity that made her say stupid things, drop entire plates of food in her own lap, and automatically punch the lights out of anyone who touched her.

83

The total for the candy was astronomical, but Gaia barely even blinked. It was worth it just for the experience. Jake held the door open for her as she maneuvered her way outside while simultaneously ripping open a bag of chocolate-covered pretzels. She bit into one and closed her eyes, savoring the taste. This had to be what happiness felt like.

"So, you up for more or do you want to head home?" Jake asked. "Cuz there's this band playing at CB's Gallery tonight. This guy Shiva from my dojo said he's seen them play. They're supposed to be pretty good."

Jake pulled a wrinkled fluorescent green flyer out of his pocket and showed it to Gaia. The ad was for a band called the Dust Magnets, and there was a scraggly line drawing of an angry-looking dust-bunny playing the guitar. The illustration looked vaguely familiar, but Gaia couldn't place it.

"Where'd you get this?" she asked, turning the page over.

"They were plastered all over Oliver's neighborhood," Jake said with a shrug. "I tore it down the other day and figured I'd check it out if I was around."

Gaia popped another pretzel into her mouth and considered the invitation. She was hardly ever home at a reasonable hour, but that was usually because she was on the lam or kicking someone's ass. But her many months of living the street urchin lifestyle had turned her into a serious night person. She wasn't remotely tired, and if she went home she was just going to sit there and obsess until her father called. Besides, now she had supplies. With the amount of food in her bag, she could go all night.

"Why not?" she said, stepping off the curb and heading for the subway. It might be cool to stay out just for fun instead of staying out to find free-lance vigilante work.

As long as it wasn't a date.

The Kicker

ED SAT BACK INTO THE CUSHY COUCH he'd managed to secure at CB's Gallery by arriving there at the very uncool hour of eight o'clock. He'd been sitting there on and off ever since, only getting up when Kai or one of her friends was there to save the seat. He figured if he was going to have to listen to Kai's brother's punk band destroy the honor and legacy of punk bands everywhere, he may as well do it from a comfortable couch.

"Hey there!" Kai said, returning from the stage where she'd been chatting with the band's drummer for the last fifteen minutes while he set up. Between the bright graphic tank top she was wearing and the glitter swept onto strategic portions of her face and shoulders, Kai was absolutely glowing. All day and all evening, Kai had been even more hyper than usual, running around, thanking everyone from school for coming. Over the past week she'd been putting up flyers advertising the gig on bulletin boards, windows, and every other empty surface she could find at the Village School.

"Miss me?" she asked, plopping down next to him.

"Yeah, totally," Ed replied, forcing a smile.

He wasn't exactly sure how to act around Kai these days. Ever since she'd basically offered her body up to him and he'd frozen faster than a shallow puddle on an Antarctic night, being with her made him tense. He was always worried she was going to try it again and he was going to bail again and she was going to start thinking he was gay. Or just really lame.

Not that she was going to undress in the middle of a crowded club, but sooner or later he was going to have to deal with the after-the-club situation.

To top it all off, it seemed that every last member of her brother's band, the Dust Magnets—minus her own brother, of course—was in love with Kai. They'd all been shamelessly flirting with her for the past hour, buying her drinks, making her laugh. And the kicker was, it didn't bother Ed in the slightest. He wasn't jealous. He wasn't proprietary. He wasn't anything.

Kai was a cool girl, but there was just `no sparkage.`

"Okay, you have contemplative face," Kai said, touching her fingertip to the top of his nose, which was wrinkled in concentration. "What's wrong?" She'd curled her black hair into a million perfect tendrils and they bounced around her face as she shifted in her seat, resting her elbow on top of his shoulder.

"Nothing," Ed replied. "Just can't wait for the music to start."

Kai's face lit up. "I know! Steve is so excited! They're totally pumping up the amps. They're going to bring this place to its knees!"

Yeah. Wailing in pain, Ed thought.

He looked at the door as he had been every time it opened, not knowing whom he expected to see, but hoping it was somebody, anybody, with whom he could share his pain. This time none other than Sam Moon walked in, followed by a horde of friends. He looked around and almost immediately spotted Ed.

Sam lifted his chin and Ed did the same, acknowledging his former nemesis in the battle for Gaia Moore's heart. Then he looked away. He knew Sam wasn't going to make pleasantries and neither was he. But seeing the guy did make Ed wonder.

What was Gaia doing tonight? And wherever she was, was she half as bored as him?

SAM GRIPPED FOUR BOTTLES OF

The Chick Stare

beer between his fingers as he carefully wove his way around tables and chairs and feet— not to mention the dozens of bags and backpacks that had been stowed on the floor. His roommate, Aidan, had found a table up near the stage with their other friends, the better to support Johnny Chen, the drummer of the band who had not only wheedled all of them into coming, but also into wallpapering their entire neighborhood in Brooklyn with those hideous green flyers. Johnny was Aidan's former roommate at NYU. They'd lived together as freshmen, hated each other as sophomores, and now that they were living in separate boroughs and hardly ever saw each other, they were best friends.

There was a whole long story involving a girl they'd fought over and a fishing trip in which they'd gotten marooned at sea, but Sam had never quite followed it. All he knew was, Aidan and Johnny were now friends and that was why he was here.

Why Ed Fargo was here was an entirely different question. Sometimes New York was entirely too small for comfort.

"Thanks, man," Aidan said as Sam placed the bottles down in the center of the imbalanced table. "What do we owe you?"

"Forget it. We'll settle up later," Sam said. He leaned his shoulder blades into the cane-backed chair and heard an ominous crack, so he sat forward again. His friends had left him a seat facing the stage, so he had to crane his neck all the way around to see Ed. Which, for some reason, was very important to him.

Because you want to see if Gaia's going to show, Sam admitted to himself. Over the past year he'd grown accustomed to admitting these things to himself.

He took a slug of his beer, then hunched his shoulders, elbows propped on the table. He turned his head slightly, making like he was just checking out the door. Ed was still sitting on the same couch with some pretty Asian girl practically straddling him. Sam smiled and turned around again.

Apparently Gaia wouldn't be making an appearance.

"So, I heard this band rocks," Jeff Miller said, already sucking the dregs from the bottom of his bottle.

"Yeah? I heard they suck," Aidan replied.

"Then why'd you make us come here?" Charlie asked.

At that moment, Johnny came down from the stage, drumsticks in one hand, mixed drink in the other. His eyes were swimming in their sockets and rimmed with red. He was a big guy, on the short side, but ripped—the kind of guy Sam would usually imagine could hold his liquor. Clearly, however, Johnny was not an accomplished drinker.

"Dude! You are the *man*!" Johnny shouted, practically tackling Aidan out of his chair as he hugged him.

"How drunk *are* you?" Aidan asked, slapping Johnny's back.

"Very. I get performance anxiety," Johnny answered over his shoulder. "But I'm so glad you're here, man!"

Aidan shot Charlie a look that said, *This is why I dragged you here.* Charlie and Jeff laughed as the hug continued, and Sam found himself looking over his shoulder again, this time toward the door.

He should have asked Gaia to come with him tonight. He'd thought about it when he'd seen her earlier, but something had stopped him. Just like something had stopped him from bringing up the messages he'd left her. And the longer he'd said nothing about it, the longer she'd said nothing about it, and the more awkward it felt to even *think* about bringing it up.

The problem was, not saying something about it made him seem like he was embarrassed about it, which he was. Too embarrassed to jump straight to asking her out.

I'm just going to have to give it some time. Not a lot. Just some, Sam thought, taking another gulp of his beer. Once the memory of the many messages had faded a bit, he'd just call her up and ask her if she wanted to get together. Do something normal. Like go to the movies or for a walk. Or maybe a game of chess in the park. That was how they'd met, after all. It would be kind of romantic.

"Earth to Sam!" Aidan said, snapping in front of his face. He was standing up next to Sam now and Johnny had returned to his seat behind the drums. "What the hell are you thinking about?"

Just wondering what Gaia's doing right now, Sam's mind replied.

"Nothing," he answered.

"You've been zoning out all day," Aidan said. "I'm surprised you figured out how to put your pants on to come here."

"It's the chick stare," Jeff said, sucking at his teeth. "He's got the chick stare."

"What the hell are you talking about?" Charlie asked with a laugh. Jeff was always saying stupid, pointless crap with this serious intonation like it was all deep.

"He's thinking about some girl," Jeff said, rather astutely for him. "It's all over his face."

Charlie, Aidan, and Jeff all looked at Sam expectantly. Like he was really going to get into a detailed conversation about his "chick stare" and the object of it with these guys in the middle of a loud club. Not likely.

"You are so off base, you're halfway to the outfield," Sam said. "I'm just trying to remember whether we remembered to pause the Xbox before we left."

"Aw, dude, you better have remembered!" Jeff cried, moving to the edge of his seat. "I was like five minutes from slaying the dragon!"

"In your dreams," Charlie said.

Sam smiled. His friends were fabulously distractable.

"So, you want another beer or what?" Aidan asked, whacking Sam's shoulder with the back of his hand.

"Still working on this one," Sam answered, tilting the bottle toward his friend.

As Aidan walked to the bar, Sam tried to tune in to Charlie and Jeff's conversation—something about the club they wanted to hit later. The band hadn't started playing yet, but the music on the sound system was still pretty loud. Sam could barely hear what anyone was saying, and he knew once the band began their set, it would become impossible. Then he could zone out all he wanted.

Zone out and think of what to say when he asked out Gaia.

GAIA LOOKED DOWN AT THE BEEFY, outstretched hand of the human boulder sitting by the door at CB's Gallery and frowned. He grunted at her.

The Usual Angst

"What?" she asked.

"You gonna pay the cover?" the guy asked, his voice a low rumble. "Ten bucks."

"Oh!" Gaia said, her face heating up instantly. She fumbled in her bag, feeling completely unsophisticated and stupid—a sensation only exacerbated when two Spider-Man lollipops fell out onto the floor. She'd never actually been inside one of these places before. How was she supposed to know what it meant when some freaky tattoo-covered bouncer grunted in her direction?

"I got it," Jake said as Gaia crouched to retrieve her candy. He'd slapped a twenty into the guy's palm before Gaia had located her wallet.

Damn, she thought as he tugged at her arm and dove into the thick crowd. *He paid again.* She was really going to have to get a handle on this stuff. Gaia's brain was brimming with street smarts, but certain way-of-the-world logic completely mystified her.

Jake made his way toward the bar and Gaia followed. Suddenly, he stopped, blocked by a tight crowd of people, and Gaia took the opportunity to get a look around. The back part of the club, by the door, was an open area with couches and tables pushed up against the walls. The room was painted white, and there was actual artwork hanging on the walls. All the little tables had votive candles flickering inside white cups.

Gaia was just noticing this when she saw a booted foot flying toward one of the candles and she instinctively went to shout a warning. But before she could get the words out, she looked up and saw that the boot belonged to that Kai girl she'd seen Ed hanging around with. And the reason it was flying toward the candle was because she was crawling all over Ed himself on a love seat near the wall.

You have to be kidding me, Gaia thought, instantly turning her face away. He hadn't seen her yet and maybe he wouldn't recognize the back of her head, what with all the uncharacteristic waves in her hair. *Of all the bars and clubs in this town, why did he have to be here?*

Suddenly, her unusual night of fun was infused with a bit more of her usual angst.

Jake finally broke through and made it to the bar and Gaia stepped up next to him, putting more bodies between herself and her ex. There was a red Dust Magnets flyer plastered to a support beam and suddenly Gaia remembered where she'd seen it before.

"These things were all over school yesterday," she said as Jake tried to get the bartender's attention.

"Yeah, like I said, they're everywhere. I think a lot of people are coming," Jake said.

You said they were everywhere in Brooklyn, Gaia thought, irritated by the triangular situation she suddenly found herself in. All she wanted to do was get the heck out of there.

Then, as the people down at the other end of the bar got their drinks and moved away, Gaia saw something that *really* made her want to get the heck out of there. Sam Moon was sitting a few yards away, staring off into space.

"Oh, come on," Gaia said out loud, her heart turning.

"I know. This guy's not giving me the time of day," Jake replied, motioning at the frazzled bartender. "What do you want, anyway?" he asked Gaia.

"Nothing," Gaia said, her pulse racing. Sam was going to turn around any second and see her here with Jake. Or Ed was going to come over to get a drink. And she really wasn't sure she could handle either of those scenarios.

What had made her think that she could get away with one normal, fun night? Didn't she know the fates were working against her here? This couldn't be a coincidence. It was *too* coincidental. Someone was definitely pulling the strings up there and he or she had a sadistic sense of humor.

"Hey, Jake? Do you think we could—"

Gaia never finished her sentence because at that moment, one of the guitars on stage let out a screech that pierced the eardrums of everyone in the room. Jake didn't hear a word of what she'd said.

A few moments later, Jake had a soda in his hand and he grabbed Gaia's wrist with the other. As they wove their way back through the crowd, Gaia saw Ed recognize them from out of the corner of her eye. And when Jake plopped down into a chair near the stage, Sam noticed them, too.

Gaia looked back through the bar toward the door, past dozens and dozens of heads that were bopping up and down to the music. She looked at Jake, whose eyes were trained on the stage. There was no way to make a fast escape. If she got up and bolted, either Jake or Ed or Sam would catch up to her before she even made it halfway to the door. Or *all* of them would. There was no doubt about it. Gaia was trapped.

Swallowing against her dry throat, she sank down as low as possible in her chair, rested her elbow on the table and shielded her face with her hand. This night was about to get interesting.

To: Y
From: X22
Subject: Damage control

Have contacted our agent within the CIA. Agent is in position to neutralize the prisoners before you can be compromised. Agent awaits your orders.

To: X22
From: Y
Subject: Re: Damage control

Negative. Neutralization is too dangerous. We must proceed carefully at this juncture.

My transfer to the new location is complete. Safe house secure. It's time to go on the offensive. Put together a team and take the girl.

"Yuri, my uncle, your beloved Katia's father, is very much alive, Tom," Natasha said firmly. "And he's here."

the bomb

ED STOOD NEAR THE WALL, BEHIND

Lost-Puppy-Dog Style

the area where the tables and chairs were set up, but in front of the crowd that was packed in behind them. Next to him, Kai bounced up and down, screaming and cheering—singing along to words that Ed couldn't remotely understand. The audience, for the most part, seemed to be enjoying the piercingly loud, repetitive set that the Dust Magnets were putting forth, but to Ed, it was torture. Every once in a while, if he could manage it without being obvious, he would press his fingertips into his ears to dull the noise and catch a bit of a reprieve.

Of course, he wasn't the only person in the room feeling tortured. Gaia was clearly ready and willing to be sucked into the ninth ring of hell. Every few seconds she seemed to be sinking a little bit lower in her chair until her knees were practically touching the ground. Jake, God bless him, was sitting slightly in front of her, watching the band, so he had yet to notice his date's—was it a date?—obvious distress.

At the same time, Sam was getting his stares in, lost-puppy-dog style. While his friends shouted and laughed to one another across the table, Sam sat back, eyeing Gaia, all droopy and sad.

Who is that guy? his look read. *Why is she here with him and not me?*

Ed had heard those thoughts in his own head more times than he cared to remember. He recognized his lost-puppy-dog expression. When it came to Gaia, he *invented* the lost-puppy-dog face. Seeing it on someone else only made him realize how pathetic he'd been for the past year. `Why hadn't somebody smacked him upside the head and told him to snap the hell out of it?`

Suddenly, Ed was struck with an idea. No one had done that for him, but that didn't mean he couldn't do it for someone else. It would be like philanthropy on a Saturday night. It might make the agony of this evening worthwhile.

"I'll be right back!" he shouted in Kai's ear. She smiled and nodded, continuing to bounce.

Ed made his way along the front of the crowd and over to Sam's table. He pulled a free chair from the next table, turned it around, and straddled it right at Sam's elbow.

"What's up, man?" Ed said.

Sam glanced at him, almost startled.

"Hey!" he shouted back with a nod. He took a sip of his beer and trained his eyes on the hideousness on the stage as if that was what he'd been watching all along.

"Look, Sam. I came over here to tell you that it's game over," Ed shouted, leaning in toward Sam's ear.

"What?" His eyebrows shot up and came together.

"Game over," Ed said, lifting his chin in Jake's direction. Sam followed his eyes, drawn back to the car wreck.

"I have no idea what you're talking about," Sam said.

But the defiant way in which he said it told Ed that he knew *exactly* what he was talking about. Still, it couldn't hurt to hammer it home.

"You see that guy she's with?" Ed said, leaning in again. "That's him. That's the guy with all the mojo you and I will never have." Ed reached up and clapped Sam on the shoulder in solidarity with his former adversary. "It's time to give it up, man," he said. "Trust me. I know."

THIS HAS TO BE OVER SOON, GAIA  thought, her head pounding as the band's front man executed some kind of wide-legged jump and almost took out the drummer's cymbals and dead-legged the bass man. *If there is any mercy in the world, this has to be over soon.*

"I'll be back in a minute!" Jake suddenly shouted at her.

Gaia sat up straight and grabbed his arm before

she could double-think it. "What? Where are you going?"

"Bathroom!" Jake yelled, starting out of his chair.

Gaia glanced in Sam's direction from the corner of her eye. Was it her imagination or was Ed just getting up from Sam's table?

"Why?" Gaia blurted.

Jake laughed. "I think it's kind of obvious. I'll be right back." Then he stepped away from the table, carefully avoiding wires and abandoned beer bottles.

Gaia suddenly felt like every light in the club was trained directly on her. *She's right here! Come and get her!*

Sam was watching her. She could feel it. She'd felt it all night long, but now it somehow seemed more intense. Her first instinct was to sink down in her chair again, but that wasn't going to get her anywhere. It wasn't going to make her disappear. Besides, her butt hurt from the edge of the seat pressing into it all night.

There was movement. Definite movement caught in her peripheral vision. Gaia cleared her throat and fixed her gaze on the band. She loved this band. She was *so* into them. She couldn't take her eyes off of them.

Yeah, right.

"Hey," Sam said, lurking just behind her shoulder. "Mind if I sit?"

Gaia pressed her lips together in a reasonable facsimile of a smile. "No extra chairs," she said pseudo-apologetically.

Sam leaned over to the couple next to them, pointing at an empty seat at their table. Seconds later, he was at eye level right across from her. Gaia glanced automatically in the direction of the bathrooms, but Jake was nowhere to be found.

"So, who's the guy?" Sam asked bluntly.

"Jake," Gaia replied, thankful that the deafening noise made it next to impossible to attempt to expand.

"Ah," Sam replied, nodding and looking around. As if the word "Jake" explained everything. He was playing it cool. Gaia could have kissed him for his male ego that required that he play it cool.

"So, listen. I've decided I'll talk to Oliver," Sam shouted, leaning in slightly.

Gaia's heart skipped a beat. "Yeah? That's great!" she shouted back.

Sam's green eyes took on new depth as he watched her face. "Yeah, well, it means a lot to you!" he yelled.

Gaia felt a stirring in her chest. So he was doing it for her. Not because he wanted to, not to help Oliver, but for her. Time for a subject change. Luckily, at that moment, the song ended, making it much easier to talk. Everyone cheered and applauded, and the front man told them all that it was time for the Dust Magnets' break.

"So," Gaia said. "I went to see Dmitri this morning."

"Yeah? I meant to ask you about that. It's weird, isn't it?" Sam said.

"What's weird?" Gaia asked.

"How he just up and split. I hope nothing's wrong," Sam said. "But then, with that guy—"

Gaia shook her head, confused. "What do you mean he up and split? I just saw him."

"Oh, he was there?" Sam said, adjusting in his seat. "Well, did he mention anything to you about where he was going, cuz he wasn't there this afternoon. . . ?"

"Sam," Gaia said, leaning forward. "What the hell are you talking about?"

"Okay, all I know is, I went over there this afternoon to get the last of my stuff, and when I got there most of Dmitri's stuff was gone—"

"And you don't know where he went?" Gaia asked, her voice rising.

"That's what I'm trying to tell you. I have no idea," Sam said. "He left me a note saying he'd be in touch and that was it."

"But I was *just* there." Gaia stood up from the table, her mind reeling. "Why didn't you call me? Why didn't you tell me this?"

"What? I just figured he was going off to do the laying low thing again," Sam said. "Ever since we busted Dmitri out he's been totally paranoid."

Gaia rolled her eyes to the ceiling and when she looked back at Sam, he seemed chagrined, like a little kid who'd just broken something expensive. "I just figured it was Dmitri being eccentric," he said. "Do you really think something's wrong?"

Gaia took a deep breath and told herself to chill. Maybe Dmitri really had gone off somewhere to stay under the radar. He'd done it before. But after the odd conversation she'd had with him that morning, something about his sudden disappearance just seemed off. Why wouldn't he have told her he was leaving?

At that moment, Jake emerged from around the corner and immediately noticed the new presence at their table. Gaia saw his face take on that territorial set as he made his way back a little faster than he'd left it. When his eyes met hers, he stopped in his tracks.

"What's wrong?" he asked, glancing down at Sam.

"We have to go," Gaia said.

"Whatever you say," Jake told her, coming around the table.

"Are you going over there?" Sam asked. "I can come if you—"

"No," Gaia interrupted a little more harshly than intended. Sam's mouth snapped shut and she instantly felt guilty. Not only was she leaving with another guy, she was rude to him in front of another guy—a major blow. Guys could be so fragile. But Gaia did not want to risk pulling Sam back into her crazy life again. "I'll let you know if we find anything," she told him.

And with that, she and Jake headed for the door.

TOM NEVER TOOK HIS EYES OFF

Natasha as he handed her the glass of water she requested. He sat down in his chair without looking at it or marking its position. He watched her and waited while she sipped from the cool, pristine glass and placed it down in front of her on the table. Tom was in charge this time. Nothing she could do or say would upset him.

"Thank you for moving Tatiana. These conversations, they're too difficult on her," Natasha said.

"You're welcome," Tom replied. He leaned back in his chair and crossed his legs, his ankle resting atop his knee. "So let's talk."

"How's Gaia?"

A surge of heat rushed up through Tom's body directly into his head. He fought the urge to glance at the one-way mirror, knowing Frenz was in there, observing him closely.

Just answer the question, Tom. No sarcasm.

"She's fine. But let's talk about you," Tom said. "For whom are you working?"

Natasha smiled slowly. "Jumping right in, Tom? You would rather not be here, I see. Is it because your colleagues gave me the deal you were so reluctant to offer?"

Tom uncrossed his legs, moved forward on his chair, and set his elbows on the table. It did bother him—the fact that his superiors had made a deal—but he wouldn't let that show. He looked deep into Natasha's eyes. "On the contrary, Natasha. There's no place I'd rather be. But you told my boss that you wanted to talk to me, and I'd appreciate it if you'd start talking."

She blinked, obviously surprised at his calm demeanor.

"Who sent you here?" he asked. "What was your primary mission? I know it wasn't to take Gaia out because you were here for months before you even attempted it."

Natasha gazed at him stonily. Tom started to lose his patience.

"Natasha, you're not stupid. You know they won't make good on your deal unless you give us some real intel," Tom said. "Why drag this out any longer? Why let Tatiana suffer any longer than she has to?"

She didn't move a muscle. She didn't even seem to be breathing. She sat like a statue for another few minutes before, finally, she opened her mouth and started to talk. Her voice was monotone, her expression resigned.

"Tom," she said. "I am Katia's cousin."

It was all he could do to keep from lifting a hand to his chest, which felt as if it had just been pierced through by a sword. Katia's cousin? *His* Katia?

"Not possible," he said, even as he saw the truth of the statement. His heart raced and he fought to control his emotions. Rosenberg and Frenz were watching, after all. He couldn't afford to lose it now.

"I know you always saw a resemblance. I know

that's why you were attracted to me. It's one of the reasons I was assigned to your case," Natasha continued in the same unaffected monotone.

It's one of the reasons I was assigned to your case. . . . This had to be wrong. This had to be a sick joke. How could anyone do this to another person—send his dead wife's cousin to seduce him—to exploit that weakness in his heart?

"Tatiana and I were sent to America to watch you. To keep an eye on you and see if you suspected what was going on within the Organization."

"The Organization," Tom repeated, adopting the same flat tone Natasha was using. If he didn't he was sure his myriad of emotions would show through, and he couldn't have that.

"You're not going to like this, Tom," Natasha said.

Tom narrowed his eyes at her. She was on the verge of telling him something. Something big. And from the triumphant look on her face, she was going to enjoy it.

"Okay, I'll bite," Tom said. "Who sent you? Who's running the Organization?"

Natasha lowered her chin and looked up at him through her lashes, her eyes gleaming. Time seemed to stop, but it hadn't. The only sound in the room was the ticking of Tom's watch.

"It is Yuri. My uncle. Katia's father. It was Yuri who sent us."

At that moment, Tom was glad to be sitting. His

every nerve and cell felt sick. Yuri Petrova could not be alive. Katia's evil psycho of a father could not be alive.

"Try again, Natasha," Tom told her, clear as a bell even as his hands shook under the table. "Yuri is six feet under and has been for years. We both know it."

"There have been many changes," Natasha continued as if Tom hadn't spoken at all. "Yuri is growing old and he needed a successor. Tatiana was being groomed to take over the Organization. But Yuri needed to be sure that you and Gaia would not get in the way. He needed to be sure that—"

Tom laughed. He couldn't help it. It was the only release he could allow himself. It burbled up through his chest and throat and pressed at his lips until he just couldn't hold it in any longer. Natasha stopped talking and stared at him.

"I'm sorry, I'm sorry," Tom said mirthfully. He pressed the top of his nose between his thumb and forefinger, then folded his hands on the table, his eyes still dancing. "It's just, I thought you were going to tell me the truth here tonight."

This couldn't be the truth. He refused to accept that.

"And I am," Natasha said blankly.

"You expect me to believe this?" Tom asked, standing abruptly, his chair scraping back across the concrete floor. He hovered over her, suddenly hyperaware of the eyes on him from the other side of the glass, hyperaware of the hammering of his own heart. "Natasha," he said, pressing his fingertips into the metal table and leaning over her. "Yuri has been dead for years."

Natasha leaned forward, the single light hanging above them casting distorted shadows across her face. She gazed up at him through her lashes, a coy smile playing on her lips. Whatever she was about to say, whatever bomb she was about to drop, she was enjoying it to the fullest.

"Yuri Petrova is very much alive, Tom," Natasha said firmly.

Tom swallowed. "I don't believe you."

"Well, you had better start," Natasha told him, cool and calm. "He is alive. And he is here."

"Here?" he repeated, searching her eyes. His body started to believe her before his brain did. The hairs on his arms stood on end and a chill shot through to his core. Natasha had lied to him before and he'd believed her, but this time she was telling the truth— the impossible, horrifying truth.

"He is in the U.S., Tom," Natasha told him, her smile widening at his obvious discomfort. "Yuri is here."

"OKAY, WHO IS THIS GUY AGAIN?" Jake asked as he and Gaia climbed the stairs in Dmitri's building two at a time. They'd given up on the

110

elevator after only two and a half minutes of waiting. Gaia and patience had parted ways hours ago.

"He's the one who helped me put Natasha in jail," Gaia told him, controlling her breathing as best she could. "And he wouldn't leave without telling me." Why would he tell her he'd always be there for her and then bolt the next minute without even a phone call? It wasn't like him.

"But that Sam guy said—"

"I know what he said," Gaia snapped, emerging onto Dmitri's floor. "And either he's wrong, or something's happened."

"Like what?" Jake asked, holding his side as he gasped for air. He was in great shape, but Gaia would bet it had been a long time since he'd taken fifteen flights of stairs at a sprint.

"I don't know! Maybe he was kidnapped! Maybe by the same people who took my father!" Gaia whispered hoarsely, growing frustrated. "That's what we're here to find out."

Gaia paused in front of Dmitri's door, took a deep breath, and knocked. There was no movement inside the apartment, no sound at all except the sound of Jake's rapid breathing behind her. She tried the knob—locked. Jake stepped aside as Gaia moved back, lifted her leg, and kicked in the door.

"Jesus!" Jake said as the locks ripped free from the wall. "Are you *trying* to get the neighbors to call the cops?"

Gaia couldn't even reply to his sarcasm. She was staring at what was left of Dmitri's apartment. This couldn't have been the same room she'd sat in just a few hours ago.

Drawers hung open, papers were strewn everywhere, a plant in the corner was overturned, a trail of clothing cut across the living room. The place was a total wreck.

"Something's not right," Gaia said flatly.

"Yeah, no kidding," Jake replied.

"Sam didn't say the place was trashed," Gaia told him, taking a couple of steps into the apartment. "He said Dmitri left a note. Somebody must have done this after Sam left."

"Like who?" Jake asked quietly.

"I don't know," Gaia said. "Someone's after him."

Then she heard a creak from a floorboard and before she could turn around, she and Jake were grabbed from behind.

You know what I need? I need
to get out of here. I don't
mean out of this bar or my
school or my apartment. I need
to get the hell out of this
city. I need a college in a
different state. Maybe a different country. I need to get
as far away from here as possible, because one thing has
become crystal clear to me: I
am never going to fall out of
love with Gaia as long as I
have to see her every damn day.
And as long as I'm still in
love with her, no other girl
has a shot. And as long as no
other girl has a shot, I've got
no shot.

No shot at love.

No shot at a functional rela-
tionship of any kind.

No shot of getting any play of
any kind on any level.

Don't get me wrong. Sex isn't
the only thing I think about.
But I am a guy. A teenage guy.
So it does occupy approximately

eighty percent of my conscious
thoughts. Maybe ninety. And when
Gaia's in the room, it's more
like ninety-nine.

When I'm with Kai, I can't
kiss her without thinking about
Gaia. And when Gaia's in my line
of vision when I'm with Kai, I
can't even focus on what the
girl is saying. I hate to admit
this, believe me. Kai deserves
better. She's an awesome girl
and I wish I could be the
boyfriend she deserves—for me
and for her. But when it comes
to girls of the non-Gaia variety
I am shit outta luck, as
they say.

So maybe if I go away—maybe
if I go to St. Louis or Seattle
or San Francisco, Paris or
Madrid or Minsk. Maybe if I
don't have to see her every day
I'll finally get her out of my
system. I'll finally be able to
focus my abundant sexual energy
on someone new. "Out of sight,
out of mind," right?

Or. . . wait . . . is it

"absence makes the heart grow fonder"?

Damn.

Why couldn't the proverb people just come up with one opinion and run with it?

"Why is Yuri here?" Tom asked. "He wants Gaia," Natasha replied.

the explanation

"SHE HAS TO BE LYING!" TOM

Credible Threat

asserted, his teeth clenched. "Yuri is dead. We know this."

Agents Rosenberg and Frenz watched Tom as he paced back and forth across the longer wall of the debriefing room. Director Vance stood in the corner, an intimidating presence, his arms crossed over his chest and his jowls working. No one present wanted Natasha's statement to be true. In his heyday, Yuri was considered to be a `credible threat` to the U.S. government. A serious danger to national security. He was on the international most wanted list. He was known for his ruthless tactics, his penchant for physical and emotional torture, his sadistic nature.

He was not a pleasant person to deal with.

"Agent Moore, I don't want to believe her any more than you do," Agent Rosenberg said, gripping her notebook. "But you and I both know she's exhibiting none of the signs of distress associated with lying. She hasn't blinked, she hasn't touched her face, she hasn't cleared her throat. We've been monitoring her body temperature with censors and—"

"I know, I know, it hasn't changed," Tom interrupted.

"And neither has her heart rate," Rosenberg finished, glancing down at her notes.

"Of course, we can't say the same for you, can we?" Agent Frenz asked stoically.

"Why don't you just say what you mean?" Tom demanded, feeling the truth of Frenz's insinuation. He was heating up even as he stood there.

"You almost lost your cool in there," Frenz pointed out. "Again."

"The woman just told me that my wife's psychotic, criminal mastermind father was still alive and that he had ordered surveillance on myself and my daughter. I think you can cut me the slightest bit of slack," Tom said, stepping up to Frenz. He was so close to the man he could see his already sizable nostrils flaring.

"Sir, I respectfully suggest that we remove Agent Moore from this case once and for all," Frenz said, taking a step back and looking at Director Vance. "I think we've given him enough chances to prove himself."

All eyes turned to Vance as he took a deep breath and rubbed his sizable hand over his face in frustration. Tom's throat was dry, but he forced himself to speak.

"I'm going back in there, sir," he said. "I have to finish this."

Vance inhaled again, drawing himself up to his full height. "Go," he said. "But tread lightly, Moore. You've been warned."

As Tom exited the room headed for the interrogation block, Frenz eyed him skeptically. Tom could have punched the little weasel.

Who the hell did he think he was, suggesting Tom step down? His rank was so far beneath Tom's, he couldn't even remember what it was like to be in Agent Frenz's position. When this debacle was over, the first thing Tom was going to do was file an inquiry into Frenz's assignment to this case. It was insulting.

Tom strode into the interrogation room and found Natasha exactly where he'd left her, sitting straight-backed at the table, waiting patiently. He sat down across from her and got down to business. He was sick of messing around.

"Why is Yuri here?" he asked.

There was a moment of silence as Natasha savored whatever morsel she was about to share. She tilted her head, sighed, looked at him like he was pitiful—like he was missing something so very obvious.

"Why, Natasha?"

"He wants Gaia," Natasha replied.

Tom felt all the muscles in his body recoil. He turned his head and looked at the one-way mirror, somehow keeping his gaze steady. He knew that Vance had his hand on the doorknob right now to come relieve him before he could explode. He tried with all his might to convey his message to his superior: *Back off. I'm staying.*

"Why?" Tom asked, his jaw clenched.

"He's decided that Gaia would be the better candidate to take over the Organization," Natasha explained.

"Tatiana has been, for lack of a better word, passed over."

I don't believe this, Tom thought, his fists gripped together under the table. *He wants Gaia? He wants Gaia to take over his international terror organization?*

"If he wants to groom her to take his place, why instruct you to kill her?" Tom managed to ask.

"He did not order the hit," Natasha replied. "That was me."

Tom once again saw himself lurching over the table. Saw himself squeezing every last trace of life out of Natasha. Instead, he waited. He breathed. He gradually started to see straight again.

"I didn't appreciate his decision to demote Tatiana. She trained all her life. She deserved to take the helm," Natasha said. She flicked something off the knee of her orange jumpsuit and gazed at Tom.

"Why did he do it?" Tom asked her. "What suddenly made him decide to. . . choose Gaia?"

"Gaia was always the ideal candidate, but Yuri couldn't risk coming to the States," Natasha explained. "Not as long as Loki was operating here. It was too risky."

Tom gazed at the tabletop, his mind working. "So once Loki fell into a coma—"

"Yuri ordered you to be taken out of the picture," Natasha finished. "I didn't know it at the time—I was as shocked as everyone else when you were taken to the hospital—but that is what he was doing. He wanted you gone so he would be free to—"

"To approach Gaia," Tom said.

"Precisely."

Tom's mind reeled. This was unbelievable. In his wildest dreams he never would have imagined that this was the story behind everything that had happened. That Yuri was alive. That the Organization still functioned under his watchful eye. That Loki. . .

"Loki had nothing to do with my kidnapping," Tom said, almost to himself.

Natasha snorted. "Of course not. It was all Yuri. Even Loki's coma. It was all orchestrated to gain access to Gaia."

She said it like it was the simplest thing in the world. Like she hadn't just told him that his own daughter—his only child—was susceptible to the world's leading psychotic. How could she do this? How could she talk to him like he was an enemy, like he was the scum on the bottom of her shoe? How could she do this to him—to *them*?

"I want proof," he said firmly. "I want proof that Yuri is still alive. Proof that you're related to Katia."

Natasha sat back in her seat, suddenly bored. "Go to the safe house in Alphabet City. Under the painting on the wall is a safe. The combination to the safe is three, twenty-two, seventeen. There will be a box inside. There you will find everything you're looking for."

Tom was out the door before she finished the sentence.

I am the worst father in the history of the earth. I brought a daughter into this world, and from the moment she took her first breath I have failed her in every conceivable way. I protected her from nothing. Quite the opposite, actually. All I've ever done is *put* her in *harm's* way.

I lost her mother. I let my insane brother worm and scheme his way into her life. Let him influence her. I left her with George Niven—an alleged friend who turned out to be a traitor. And then I left her with Natasha, who not only tried to kill her, but who was working for a man who wants to take her and groom her to become head of one of the most evil institutions ever known to man.

My daughter grew up not only without parents, but having to face the worst possible threats on a daily basis. Not only did she have to deal with the normal

anxieties of adolescence—boys,
school, friends—but she had to
fight off my enemies. She had to
fight for her life every day and
I wasn't there to comfort her, to
guide her, to give her a shoulder
to cry on.

I'm a sham.

If this turns out to be true—
if Yuri is alive—I have to take
him out. He will not have my
daughter. I don't care if I have
to move her to Alaska or
Australia or the Amazon. But this
time, I will protect her. I will
do whatever it takes.

Even if I die trying.

"GET AHOLD OF HER, DAMN IT!

Grab her around the arms!"

Resignation

"She's freakin' strong, man!"

"She's just a girl, for Christ's sake!"

The muffled voices came through the dark shroud that had been yanked over Gaia's head. She struggled and fought against the viselike grip of the man who held her, kicking her legs out, flailing back and forth, but it was no use. She was being dragged backward toward the door, off her feet, the heels of her boots squeaking against the hardwood floor.

What the hell is going on? Gaia wondered. Were these the same people that had taken Dmitri? And kidnapped her father? How had they known she would be here? They had, after all, come prepared. They had black sacks for blindfolding and a precision uncommon to run-of-the-mill burglars and drug fiends that might prey on a recently deserted apartment.

Yep. This was planned. Planned, of course, for her. The resignation settled over Gaia's shoulders like a steel blanket. Someone was still after her and they had anticipated she would come looking for Dmitri. Whoever they were, she'd walked right into their grasp.

Gaia heard Jake sputtering and cursing and struggling somewhere in the darkness and she was suddenly thrown to the floor. Her spine was slammed against the hard surface and `a foot pressed into her sternum.`

"Jake?" she called out, coughing against her will. "Jake, where the hell are you?"

"I'm right here," Jake's voice replied. He was still standing—somewhere over her. And he sounded like he was trying not to sound scared.

"Not for long," one of the voices said with an obvious sneer. "Kill the kid. We don't need him."

Gaia took a sharp inhale as a rush of adrenaline burst through her veins. She reached up into the darkness, grabbed the ankle attached to the foot that pinned her down, and flung it left with all her might. The guy went down hard, kicking her in the jaw as he went, but the rest of the attackers were surprised enough to give her a few seconds.

She jumped to her feet and whipped the black sack off her head. Jake was pinned against the living room wall, his arms tied behind him, the barrel of a gun pressed into his forehead. Gaia saw the gun-bearer's thumb pull back the safety.

"Duck!" she shouted.

Jake hit his knees and Gaia, aware that there were three other men converging on her from all sides, tackled the gunman to the ground. The firearm skittered under one of Dmitri's massive bookcases and the attacker looked up at her, stunned. Gaia brought her fist down right in the center of his face, knocking his head back against the floor. His whole body went limp as he fell unconscious.

"Gaia! What the hell is going on?" Jake shouted.

Gaia turned around and saw all three of the other men advancing on her slowly, arms outstretched, like she was a rabid lion. At that moment she felt like one. These guys had messed with the wrong girl at the wrong moment on the wrong night. They were about to feel a lot of pain.

"Don't do anything stupid," the guy in the center said.

They were all wearing black ski masks with just the eyes cut out, but this guy's eyes were the kind of extremely light blue that was almost clear. The skin around them was pale and his eyebrows were so blond they were barely visible. He was scrawny. Too scrawny to take her unless he had some serious skills.

My first target, Gaia thought, nearly salivating.

She bent at the waist and rushed the guy, flying right past his two friends and tackling him onto the glass coffee table, which shattered all around them. She pinned him down with both hands to his neck and reached up with her back leg to kick one of the advancing attackers in the face. He flew back into a bookcase and didn't get up again. Then the guy beneath her lifted both legs and kicked her over his head, where she tumbled awkwardly into the side of

Dmitri's favorite chair before quickly scrambling to her feet.

"Gaia, I can help if you'd just—"

She whirled over to Jake, who had struggled to his feet, and whipped off his blindfold. He looked relieved to see her alive, but that lasted less than a second. His eyes widened and Gaia instinctively ducked at the same moment Jake did. A huge vase shattered against the wall right where their heads had been.

"My hands," Jake said, crouched to the floor.

Gaia tugged at the cloth that bound his wrists and, surprisingly, it came apart easily. When they stood up again, it was two on two. Scrawny Guy and his bigger buddy faced them down, but being against the wall, Jake and Gaia were at a distinct disadvantage.

Suddenly, Scrawny Guy let out a battle cry and rushed Jake. Jake ducked his punch yet again and Scrawny Guy cracked his knuckles against the exposed brick wall, crying out in pain. Gaia saw the blood out of the corner of her eye.

So maybe the wall *wasn't* a bad thing.

She and Jake exchanged a look and the battle began.

Gaia attacked the bigger guy with a flurry of punches, ducking and weaving anything that he tried to counter with. He was slow, but she could tell that if one of those right hooks hit home, she could be down for the count. Gaia concentrated her power on his head, hoping to knock him out the same way she'd knocked out his friend. But suddenly, there was a crash off to her left, and Gaia turned to see if Jake was all right.

Big mistake.

Jake was fine—it was the Scrawny Guy who was down and struggling to get up, `having taken a potted plant to the head.` But when Gaia turned around again, there was a fist coming right at her face.

Uh-oh, Gaia thought.

Her eye exploded in pain. Sparks seemed to flash across her plane of vision as she sprawled across the floor. Her cheekbone felt as if it had just been smashed with a tire iron.

Head pounding, Gaia flipped over onto her back and saw a boot coming for her gut. It was about to hit home when she rolled away, gaining as much momentum as she could. She slammed into the bookcases and grabbed a shelf to leverage herself up, but she was only halfway to standing when the same boot hit her squarely in the center of her lower back.

"Stay down, bitch!" the guy said.

She could hear Jake and Scrawny Guy, still duking it out behind her as she tried to catch her breath. Scrawny turned out to have more stamina than she'd thought. The bigger guy backed away from her to help his associate, seemingly satisfied that she would take his advice. That was when she saw it: the gun handle, sticking out ever so slightly from under the bookcase.

Gaia grabbed it and whirled around as she stood, still regaining control of her breathing. She pulled back the safety and aimed.

"Don't move!"

The big guy stopped in the middle of the living room and Scrawny Guy looked at her like a deer caught in headlights. Jake hit him with one swift elbow to the back of the head, knocking him out. Then he walked over, crunching across the broken glass on the floor, and stood next to Gaia, never taking his eyes off hers.

"Turn around," she told the last man standing.

He did as he was told, arms raised to shoulder height out at his sides.

"Don't do anything stupid, kid," he said, eyeing the gun.

"Who sent you?" Gaia spat. Her hand started to shake and she reached up with her other arm to steady herself.

"Like I'm gonna tell you that," he said.

"I think you will," Gaia said, taking a few steps toward him. She was starting to feel weak. Her head was getting groggy. It was coming and it was coming on fast.

No. Not yet, she begged. *Not until I find out what is going on.*

Her eyes stung with unshed tears as her hands continued to tremble with exertion. She thought it was over.

She thought she was free. Who the hell was trying to kidnap her now?

"Tell me!" Gaia said through her teeth, struggling to ward off the blackness.

"Gaia," Jake said.

"Look, you're gonna have to shoot me. Cuz I tell you, and I'm dead, anyway," the guy said, smirking.

"All right. Enough is enough."

Jake walked around behind the thug and took him down the same way he'd taken out Scrawny Guy. Gaia let her arms go limp. As her knees went out from under her, her mind was racing.

Who took Dmitri? Who's after me? Who. . . ?

Suddenly she felt Jake's arms around her, stopping her fall. He lowered her to the floor and sat cross-legged with Gaia across his lap. The darkness was coming more intensely now, enveloping her, dragging her down. She felt him slip the gun from her fingers and she tried to speak, but it was too late.

Right before she blacked out she felt the touch of his lips against her forehead.

TOM WAITED IN THE HALLWAY, HIS

back up against the wall as the tactical team swept the premises of  **All True**

Natasha's safe house. His patience grew thin, even though he'd only been there no more than two minutes. He needed to get inside. He had to get inside.

He couldn't believe that any of the things Natasha had told him were true—not until he saw proof with his own eyes.

Kurt Handler, the squad leader, stuck his helmeted head out of the apartment and flipped up his clear eye-guard. "We're all clear, sir," he said.

"Get them out of there!" Tom told him. "I don't want anything moved."

Handler pressed a button on the side of his helmet and spoke into the built-in microphone. "Blue team, move out!" he said. Seconds later, half a dozen agents tromped out of the apartment and headed back down the stairs. Only Handler stayed behind, guarding the door with his M-16.

"It's all yours, sir," he said with a nod.

Tom's hands were clammy as he slipped past Handler into the small apartment. It was sparsely furnished, the walls painted a bland white, but he didn't take in much detail. A forensics team could comb the place later. For now, all he cared about was the safe.

He picked the framed poster off the wall and revealed a small door. As he worked the combination, his fingers were calm and sure, as they'd been trained to be for so many years, but he was barely breathing. This was it. The moment of truth.

The door swung open with a creak, and inside Tom found stacks of currency from countries all over the world, along with a dozen or more passports from various nations. He pushed everything aside and felt the back of the safe for the box. The box she'd said would be there. The box he almost hoped he wouldn't find.

His fingers grazed a sharp edge and Tom's heart froze. He grasped a small metal box and pulled it out, being careful not to disturb the other contents of the safe. When he opened the box his knees felt slightly weak. He walked over to the ratty couch and sat down.

There, right on top of a stack of photos, was a picture of two young girls, smiling with their arms wrapped around each other. One he recognized immediately. The blond hair, the wide grin, the dimple in one cheek, the gold lavaliere necklace hanging around her slim neck.

Katia. She looked so much like Gaia had at that age, she was like a double of her daughter.

And the other girl was undoubtedly Natasha. Her hair darker and fuller, her smile more reserved, her eyes mischievous. There was no doubt in his mind that he was looking at a younger version of the woman he'd interrogated earlier that night.

Also obvious in the photo was the resemblance between the two girls. The high cheekbones, the sloped noses, the set of their eyes. They had their differences, but they were clearly related. Cousins. No doubt about it. They could have been sisters.

Reluctantly, Tom flipped to the next photo in the pile and his mouth went dry. The same two girls, same day, but this time Yuri was in the picture. His face smiled out from between the heads of the two girls, his hands wrapped around their shoulders. A family.

It was all Tom could do to keep from crushing the photos in his hand.

From there, he knew what he would find. There were pictures of Natasha and Tatiana through the years. Pictures of Tatiana growing up, riding horses, practicing archery, firing a gun. And then, the very last photo was the one Tom was looking for but hoping he wouldn't find. His blood ran cold as he lifted it and held it up to the light.

Yuri. No doubt about it. He was older, grayer, and more frail but had the same cold, determined look on his face that Tom remembered so well. He had his arm around Tatiana, who gazed stoically at the camera, her palm pressed into the barrel of a rifle that stood in front of her. In the photo, Tatiana was only a year or so younger than she was now.

Yuri was alive. `Everything Natasha had told him was true.`

Tom dropped the picture back into the box, slammed the lid shut, and headed for the door. He had to find Gaia. He had to find her *now*.

JAKE SAT DOWN GINGERLY ON THE

Irrevocably Stupid

couch next to Gaia and pressed a bag of frozen green beans against her cheek. Gaia winced, a shot of pain streaming right through her temple, then reached up and took the bag, holding it in place. Jake pulled away and leaned forward to study her face, his brow creased. She couldn't even imagine what the bruise looked like, considering how tender and puffy it felt.

"You know, with the lives you Moores lead, you might want to stock fresh steaks in your fridge," Jake said with mock-seriousness.

Gaia scoffed and the pain radiated along her jawbone. She grimaced and closed her eyes. That guy packed even more power in his punch than she'd imagined.

"Sorry. I won't make you laugh again," Jake said, raising his hands. His perfect face was unscathed except for a small scrape on the underside of his chin.

Gaia was just leaning back into the couch, ready to collapse and really *focus* on her new obsession over who might be chasing her, when the door to the apartment burst open. Her father barreled in, his hair sticking up slightly on top, panic radiating from him like visible energy. Gaia sat up straight again and Jake instantly got to his feet. The moment Gaia's father saw them, his entire demeanor changed. His shoulders lowered from up by his ears back to their normal position.

"You're here. Thank God," he said. Then he came around the coffee table and saw Gaia with the frozen food package against her face. His Adam's apple bobbed up and down as he checked his emotions. "What happened?"

"We got jumped," Jake replied.

"By professionals," Gaia added, moving her jaw around to see if she could. It hurt a little too much so she closed her mouth again.

"Damn it," Tom said, turning away from them. He brought his hand to his face and Gaia looked up at Jake. What was going on?

"You know who did it, don't you?" Gaia asked, ignoring the little aching shoots around her cheekbone.

"I have my suspicions," Tom said. He hung his head for a moment and then took a deep breath. There was a heavy sense of foreboding in the air. Something bad was about to happen. Her father turned around again and looked her in the eye. "You're not going to like this," he said.

"Shocker," Gaia said under her breath. Jake sat down next to her, sitting a bit closer. For a moment Gaia thought he was going to reach for her hand again, but he didn't. Instead he pressed it into his thigh as if he was concentrating to keep it there.

Gaia's father sat down at her other side, a few inches away so that he could turn to face her. Gaia held her breath and pushed the frozen beans a little more firmly into her face, bracing herself.

"Gaia, Yuri. . . your grandfather. . . is alive."

Gaia blinked. "Mom's dad?"

"And this is a bad thing, I take it?" Jake put in.

Tom shot him a look that told him to keep out of this discussion. Gaia quickly decided to check her tongue as well. There had to be a good story behind this. Back when Yuri was alive he was a serious menace—a person her mother had gone to the ends of the earth to escape. Loki supposedly murdered him years ago. This revelation was just one more sud in the soap opera of Gaia's life, but it was a big one.

Tom quickly recounted the story—Gaia heard all about Natasha's confession and the information and the confirmation. She took it all in, going a little more numb with each word that was spoken.

"So Natasha wanted me dead because she thought I was going to take Tatiana's job," Gaia said slowly, when her father was through.

"Basically," Tom said. "But it's not just a job. It's a lot more than that. *A lot* more."

"Yeah, I get that," Gaia said.

"So there's some freak out there positioning himself

to kidnap her and train her to be the head of an international terrorist cell?" Jake asked.

How keen, Gaia thought sarcastically. She couldn't believe she was having this conversation. Couldn't she ever just have a talk with her father about the weather, her grades, the messy state of her bedroom?

"I took a few of the pictures," Tom told her, reaching into the breast pocket of his suit jacket. "Was this man there tonight when you were attacked? I doubt he'd come himself, but you never know."

Gaia took the picture from her father and her brow creased in confusion. "What's Tatiana doing with Dmitri?"

"Dmitri?" her father asked. "Who the hell is Dmitri?"

Gaia's mouth went dry. She had a feeling she knew what was coming, but the very idea, the very *thought* made her feel so indescribably, indubitably, irrevocably stupid, she wished there was some way to shut her ears against hearing it. But she couldn't, so instead, she closed her eyes.

And then, her father said the words she wanted least to hear. "Gaia, this man's name is not Dmitri," he told her. "It's Yuri."

Why can't things be different? I know. . . I know. . . everyone in the world wishes things were different, but I don't understand. I don't understand what went wrong.

Well, that's not exactly right, is it? I do understand what went wrong. I had a disease. I had treatments. I developed a disorder. And that disorder was responsible for atrocities I will never be able to reconcile myself with. That atrocity killed people. It killed a lot of people. It killed the woman I loved. And yes, these things are hard to bounce back from. Nearly impossible. To ask someone to forgive what I've done. . .

But that's just it. *I* didn't do those things. It wasn't me. It was him. It was all him. And if there's one person who should understand that, it should be my brother. He was there. He saw it all—what I went through as a young boy, how I changed as I grew into a man. He of all people should know that I have no control over Loki's actions. He of all people should *know*.

I wish he would die. I wish he would just wither and sputter and die.

Not my brother. No. Not Tom. Of course. But Loki. Why won't he die? Why won't he go away and leave me alone? Why do I have to live with this? What did I do? Where did I go wrong? Am I being punished for some crime in a past life? Is this some kind of test? Twins are born, one perfectly normal and blessed, the other mad and cursed? Is this my test?

At least Gaia knows. At least Gaia can forgive. And she's the last person I would have expected it from. She's just so young. How can she understand? How can she forgive the person who murdered her own mother?

But it wasn't me. Not me. Not me. Him.

I need my family back. I need them. Don't they see that I need

them? I need someone to ground me.
To stay with me. To talk to me
and. . . and. . . to *see* me. See
me and not him. If they won't let
me. . . if they won't come. . .
then how can . . . how can I. . .

    This struggle. It's too much.
How can I. . .

    But it wasn't me. It was him.
It wasn't me.

    Why won't they let me in? Why. . .
why. . . why. . . ?

He couldn't stop thinking about the fact that she was out there somewhere **guys** **like** with that Jake **him** jerk, possibly doing things that he didn't even want to think about.

ABOUT HALFWAY THROUGH THEIR
second set, Sam decided it was
time to bail on the Dust
Magnets. He hadn't imbibed as
much alcohol as his buddies
had, and his judgment was still
intact. To him, the Dust
Magnets' music sounded much
like the soundtrack the
devil might play in
hell.

The Female Spectrum

Sam walked toward the subway, his thoughts gradually turning toward Gaia and her new boyfriend—if that's what he was. He definitely didn't seem like Gaia's type. Sam thought Gaia went for the more intelligent, laid-back, scruffy-around-the-edges type. Guys like him.

But then, he knew firsthand that it was possible to be attracted to two very different people at the same time. Look at his own track history: He'd moved right from Heather Gannis to Gaia Moore. Those two occupied completely opposite ends of the female spectrum.

So maybe she does still have feelings for me, Sam thought as he approached the entrance to the F train. *If she does, I know I can still win her back.* The problem was, he couldn't stop thinking about the fact that she was out there somewhere with that Jake jerk, checking up on Dmitri—Dmitri, who was *Sam's* friend. Sam should have been the one helping Gaia. Jake had nothing to do with it and yet he'd run out of the club with her as if it was his place—his job.

As if he was Gaia's boyfriend.

Sam's heart turned as he tried to blot out the mental images that threatened to take over—Gaia and Jake holding hands, Gaia and Jake kissing, Gaia and Jake going back to her apartment. . . .

He had never felt quite this jealous in his life.

It was time to get home and go to bed and put an end to this awful night. In the morning, the situation would look brighter. In the morning, he could come up with a plan to get back into Gaia's life. Sam was about to descend the steps to the subway station when he heard his cell phone ringing. He grabbed it out of his jacket pocket and checked the caller ID screen, smiling when he saw Gaia's name and number.

See? She can't stay away, he told himself.

Stepping away from the subway entrance so a pack of people could squeeze by, Sam hit the talk button and lifted the phone to his ear.

"Hey, Gaia. What's up?" he said.

"Sam, are you sure Dmitri didn't tell you where he was going?" Gaia demanded. Her tense tone of voice made all the hair on Sam's arms stand on end.

"Whoa, slow down. Are you okay?" Sam asked.

"What did he say the last time you saw him? I need specifics," Gaia said.

Sam's brow creased as he leaned back against the

low wall surrounding the subway entrance. "Uh. . . not much. We mostly talked about me. . . my new place. . . my new job. . . ."

"Just think for a second. Did he say *anything* about where he might be?" Gaia asked impatiently.

"No. Nothing," Sam said, pushing himself up straight again. "Did you try calling him?"

"His cell phone was disconnected."

"Gaia, what's going on?" Sam asked. "Is Dmitri in danger?"

He heard her draw in a breath and then blow it out right into the speaker—right into his ear. "Listen, this is really important," she said. "If Dmitri contacts you, try to find out where he is and don't, I mean *do not* tell him where *you* are, okay?"

Her voice was full of concern. Concern for him. But why? Dmitri was their friend. He'd done nothing but help them since the day they'd met him—the day they'd found him held captive in the same compound Sam had called home for months. What did they have to fear from Dmitri?

"Gaia," Sam said, lowering his voice as a couple strolled slowly by. "You have to tell me what's going on. What did Dmitri do?"

"I can't get into it right now, but you have to trust me. The man is dangerous," Gaia said. "I can't believe I let him get so close to us."

Sam swallowed hard. Gaia sounded upset—more

upset than he'd heard her sound since her father went missing. He felt his protective nature kick in.

"Is there anything I can do?" he asked, gripping the phone. "Do you want me to come over?"

"No, it's okay," Gaia replied. "I have to go. Just. . . call me if you hear from him."

"Okay," Sam said.

But Gaia never heard it. The line was already dead. Sam swore under his breath and turned off the phone, feeling suddenly helpless and trapped. How could she just call him and say all those things to him with no explanation? He'd been *living* with Dmitri for weeks, for God's sake. What had he done to put Gaia so far over the edge?

There's nothing you can do, a little voice in his mind told him. *She'll come to you if she needs you.*

But the thought was small comfort. For as long as he'd known Gaia Moore, Sam had never seen her come to anyone for help.

"LET ME MAKE SURE I HAVE THIS

Actual Tears

right—Sam Moon was *living* with Yuri?" Tom blurted, pacing back and forth in front of the coffee table.

Gaia and Jake sat on the couch,

looking like two wide-eyed little kids that were being scolded by their father. They watched him warily, like they were afraid that at any moment he might spontaneously combust and take them with him. He didn't blame them. He *felt* like he was about to explode.

"We didn't know he was Yuri," Gaia told him for the fifth time in as many minutes. "He passed himself off as one of Loki's prisoners."

"This is insane. It's just insane," Tom said, his mind reeling. "And you're telling me he helped you capture Natasha?"

Gaia nodded slowly. "He tipped off the CIA. Why would he help the good guys?"

"Well, Natasha tried to kill you," Jake pointed out. "And from what your dad said, it seems like this Yuri guy wouldn't have wanted that to happen."

"Exactly," Tom said, finally pausing in his maniacal pacing. "Once Natasha became a threat to his plans he just gave her up."

"But Dmitri was trying to help me find you," Gaia said, tossing the bag of vegetables she'd been toying with onto the table. "He sent me into this travel agency. . . this front for the Organization to find information on where you were being held."

Tom watched his daughter's mind work as she trailed off, clearly trying to put two and two together. He couldn't have imagined the cocktail of emotions she was experiencing at that moment. He was so proud of her—she was so brave, so intelligent, so resilient. But at the same time, he was frightened for her.

I have to get her out of here, he thought again. *Take her somewhere where Yuri can't find her. This can't go on.*

"But I never found any information," Gaia said finally, pressing her hand into her forehead. "I stole that other file he wanted, but there was nothing on you. Why would he send me on a covert mission to steal from his own organization?"

"A travel agency, you said?" Tom asked, sitting in one of the chairs across the coffee table. "Was it a little place downtown? Between a shoe store and a computer repair shop?"

"Yeah. . . ," Gaia said slowly.

"That's not a front for the Organization, it's a front for the CIA," Tom told her, his stomach curling in on itself. "Yuri sent you in to steal from the CIA."

A thick silence descended over the room and Tom had to swallow back actual tears of frustration. The very thought of the danger that man had put his daughter in—the idea of him manipulating her and Sam into thinking he was some innocent victim— made Tom so ill he wanted to crawl out of his skin.

"Do you remember what it was?" Tom asked.

"Just a file. I never looked at it," Gaia said, slumping back into the couch, dazed. "I can't believe I was so stupid."

"There's no way you could have known," Jake

said before Tom could get out the exact same words. He looked at Jake gratefully. Tom was starting to like this kid.

"Gaia, I think we need to get you out of here," Tom said, leaning forward. He rested his elbows on his thighs and pressed his hands together. "I want you safe. That's all I care about."

"Dad, no," Gaia said firmly, sitting up again. Her blond hair fanned out over her shoulders, framing her beautiful, determined face. "No. I am *not* leaving you."

The tears behind his eyes intensified at her words, but he once again fought them back.

"Gaia—"

"Dad, no," Gaia repeated. She stood up and took a few steps toward the end of the couch, pushing her hands into her hair. "I am not going to run," she said, turning to him. "I've never run before and I'm not going to start now."

"Gaia, you know I'm all for fighting this guy, but maybe your dad's right," Jake said, turning in his seat so he could face her. "This Yuri guy sounds like he doesn't mess around. They almost killed both of us tonight."

"I know," Gaia said. "That's why we have to end this—now. Just think about it, Dad. We bring Yuri to justice and it's over. He's the last link. Loki is gone. . . . If we take Yuri down it'll actually be over."

Tom let her words sink in and felt a flutter of

something new within him. Hope, maybe. Determination, definitely. Gaia was right. With Yuri out of the way and Loki squelched, the Organization would crumble. The last threats to his daughter's life would be obliterated.

But he didn't like the fact that she kept using the word "we."

"I know what you're saying, Gaia," he said, rising out of his chair. "But if Yuri is going to be taken out, you are going to be far, far away when it happens."

"How can you say that?" Gaia asked, whirling around to face him fully. Her eyes flashed, reminding him of the way Katia reacted whenever he picked an argument with her. "Dad, this is our fight. This man is my *grandfather*. He's Mom's father and he betrayed me. He betrayed us all. How can you even think about calling in some team to take care of him? We *have* to do this ourselves."

"Not without some backup," Tom argued. "I don't think you appreciate exactly how dangerous this man is."

"I do," Gaia said, drawing herself up straight. "But we have an edge. We know where he was staying and he left in a hurry. He must have tripped up—left something behind that could help us."

Tom sighed and shook his head. "We can't go in alone," he told her. "You already got jumped there once. He may have sent more operatives."

"But this time we'll be prepared for that," Gaia said.

"I'll come with you," Jake said suddenly, standing as well. Tom saw his jaw working beneath his skin as he crossed his sizable arms over his chest. "I want to help."

Gaia's mouth twitched into a smile that she quickly banished. "We should get Oliver, too," she said, looking Tom in the eye. "Now that we know he had nothing to do with this, he could be good to have around."

Tom's shoulder muscles coiled and he looked away. The very idea of talking to Oliver was almost too much for him to handle. He was going to have to apologize. He saw that now. But even though he'd been cleared in this matter, Tom still didn't trust his brother. He wasn't sure if he'd ever trust the man completely.

When he glanced back at Gaia again, her gaze was unwavering—steadfast. Whether or not Tom trusted his twin, Gaia clearly did. And she was right. Checkered past or no, Oliver's skills would be helpful in this particular operation. It was time for Tom to swallow his pride and call his brother.

"Fine," Tom said finally, trying to ignore the sick feeling that permeated his heart. He crossed to the table next to the couch and reached for the phone. "Let's get this over with."

OLIVER STRAIGHTENED HIS COLLAR

The First Step

and smiled contentedly as he lifted his fist to rap on Tom and Gaia's door. He'd been most surprised when the phone had trilled in the middle of the night and even more surprised to hear his twin's voice on the other end, asking him to come in to the city ASAP. It was an odd time of day for a reconciliation, but beggars can't be choosers.

The door flew open and Oliver blinked, startled. Gaia stood there in a T-shirt and a Kevlar vest, her face flushed and her eyes filled with a sort of grim excitement.

"What's going on?" Oliver asked automatically.

"We have a lot to tell you," Gaia said, stepping aside to let him pass.

Oliver walked slowly into the living room, his mind working double time. At the same moment, Tom stalked in from the hallway, pressing a gun into a hip holster. His button-down shirt was open to reveal his Kevlar vest. Jake stood in the corner by the window, talking into a cell phone. There was an almost palpable energy in the air.

"Ollie," Tom said, lifting his chin. "We need to talk."

Oliver felt his pulse quicken in a way he relished. He followed his brother into a bedroom down the hallway and waited as Tom closed the door. He almost didn't dare to hope.

"Is everything all right, Tom?" Oliver asked.

"No. No, everything is not all right," Tom said, looking him in the eye. There was still caution there, but something had changed. His brother was no longer afraid. "Oliver, I know it wasn't you who kidnapped me. I know you had nothing to do with the hit on Gaia. And I want you to know. . ."

This was difficult for his brother, Oliver could tell. He ached to hear the words, but he didn't prompt them. He had waited a long time for this moment. He could wait until Tom was ready.

"I want you to know that I'm sorry," Tom said finally, his voice husky. "I think you understand why I couldn't fully trust you in Russia, but I'm sorry for how I treated you."

"It's all right," Oliver said, somehow containing the maelstrom of emotions within him. "You had a lot to process."

"Yes," Tom said, tucking his hands under his arms. "To be honest, I still do."

"Of course," Oliver told him, refusing to let his brother's continued wariness get to him. This was a start. A first step. It was all he could ask for.

"But I'm glad to have you back, brother," Tom said, unexpectedly. His voice actually cracked. "It's good to have you back."

Shocked by this sudden effusion of emotion, Oliver was hardly prepared when his brother enveloped him in an awkward, stiff—but still heartfelt—hug. Oliver slapped his brother's back and quelled a wave of tears that threatened to take over. This was it. The moment he'd hoped for. The moment he'd lived for.

The Moore brothers were back.

Oliver pulled away from Tom and clasped his shoulder. Neither was comfortable with outpourings of emotions. They'd done what they needed to do and there was clearly some other serious business at hand.

"Why don't you tell me what's going on? Why is your daughter out there in a bulletproof vest?" Oliver asked.

Tom took a deep breath and blew it out noisily. "Well, Ollie. . . You up for a mission?"

"Absolutely," Oliver said, following Tom back out to the living room/dining room area. Gaia was laying equipment out on the table while Jake was still over by the window, his back to the room as he spoke into the phone. "Who wants to tell me what's going on?" Oliver asked, pushing his hands into his pockets.

Gaia shot a look at her father. "You might want to sit down for this," she told Oliver, twisting her hair back into a messy bun. But Oliver stood stock-still. He was feeling fairly euphoric after his talk with Tom. Nothing could bring him down.

"Okay," she said with a shrug. "Remember Yuri? He's alive. We have to get him."

Oliver pulled a chair out from the dining room table and fell into it. "That's not possible," he said. "Yuri's dead. Loki shot him. I remember it like it was yesterday."

"Yeah, well, Loki got duped," Tom said, buttoning up his shirt. Any trace of emotion was gone as he was back to business. "And now Yuri's after Gaia."

Oliver's heart skipped a long beat as he gazed up at his niece, his mind reeling. "This doesn't make any sense," he managed to say.

"I know, but we don't have time to figure it out right now," Gaia told him. "I know the last apartment he was staying in. We're going there to see what we can find."

Oliver watched as Tom helped Jake into a bullet-proof vest and showed him how to fasten the shoulder straps. Gaia pulled a sweatshirt on over her own vest. Her hair stuck out in all directions from the static. They looked like they were getting ready for battle.

But with Yuri? It couldn't be. All these years Loki had been running the Organization—feared, revered, respected. And he'd only been able to do it by murdering Yuri—by showing everyone who the new boss was. What had Yuri been doing all that time? If Oliver knew anything about the man, he knew that he couldn't have been just sitting around twiddling his thumbs. Yuri loved the Organization—it was his baby. He must have hated Loki for taking it away. He must have been plotting revenge.

"Will you come with us?" Gaia asked.

Oliver swallowed hard. "Of course I will." His family needed him. He would go wherever they asked. It was just going to take him a little while to process all of this. It was as if the whole world order had shifted in the space of three seconds.

"Oliver? Are you okay?" Gaia asked.

"I'm fine," Oliver said, clearing his throat, trying to banish thoughts of Yuri and what he might want to do to the man who had tried to take his life.

"Where did you get all this equipment?" Oliver asked, picking up a stun gun and inspecting it. He had to put thoughts of his own safety out of his mind. This was about protecting Gaia and Tom. It was time to focus.

"I kept it in a locker in storage," Tom said. He picked up the last vest from the table and handed it to Ollie. "Good thing, too. Who knew I'd need it for something like this?"

"Well, you were always the smart one," Oliver half joked.

He slipped into the vest and zipped up the front, glancing at Gaia, who smiled back at him. Oliver's heart warmed. Suddenly he felt like part of the family again—part of a team. And for once, he was on the right side.

"All set?" Gaia asked, looking at Jake over Oliver's shoulder.

"Yeah. I talked to my dad," Jake said, yanking a sweater on over his head as he approached them. "I'm good to go."

"Gaia?" Tom asked.

"Ready," she replied with a nod.

"Ollie?"

Oliver pulled his jacket on over his vest and nodded, determined. "Let's do it."

To: Y
From: X22
Subject: Genesis

Capture unsuccessful. Please advise: X22

To: X22
From: Y
Subject: Re: Genesis

You stupid, blithering idiot! How could you
fail to catch one small girl? I know she is
powerful, but I told you this. I warned you. How
many men did you send in? Did you not bring
weapons? Are you that idiotic?

I would like you to proceed by sitting on your
hands while I get this done right. Continue
reports on Cain and Abel. Don't screw up again.

Visions of his body being flung across the room, of a giant fireball exploding out the side of the building, of Gaia's limp, dead form, flashed across his mind's eye.

jake the spy

JAKE FLATTENED HIMSELF UP AGAINST

The Roller Coaster

the wall of the hallway outside Yuri's apartment, feeling once again like he was in the middle of a Vin Diesel movie. After what had happened here the last time, he had expected to be peeing in his pants from fear, but he was strangely calm— excited, but calm. Maybe he was getting used to this stuff. Maybe he even had a future in the spy game.

How cool would that be? Jake thought, trying not to smile. This was not an appropriate situation for smiling.

Tom signaled to Jake and Gaia to stay put and stay quiet, then nudged open the broken door with his toe. He took a few steps inside, inspecting the area. Jake glanced at Oliver, who gazed back, his cool blue eyes telling Jake to take it easy—be patient.

Suddenly Tom reappeared in the doorway.

"Let's go," he whispered.

The team tromped through the door and into the apartment. Jake paused before entering, looking both ways down the hall to see if anyone was lurking, but there was no movement.

When Jake walked into the apartment, Gaia, Oliver, and Tom were standing in the living room, taking in the scene. Blood dotted the floor around the smashed coffee table. The men he and Gaia had knocked out, however, were all gone.

"Fan out," Tom said, sweeping his arm toward Jake and Gaia. "I want to get this over with. Bring us anything that looks suspicious."

"I got the bedroom," Jake said, heading for a closed door near the back of the apartment. Oliver followed as he carefully stepped over a few bills and envelopes on the carpet, in case they were important, and grasped the brass doorknob. He opened the door and was about to walk in when he heard a click and a beep.

"Stop!" Oliver shouted, causing Jake's heart to jump.

Jake was about to pull his hand away from the doorknob, but Oliver touched his arm, stopping him.

"Don't move a muscle," he told Jake.

Jake swallowed with difficulty. He wanted to ask what the hell was going on, but he was afraid to open his mouth. Oliver dropped to the ground, turned on his side, and slid through the space between Jake's legs and the door.

"What's going on?" Tom asked, approaching them with Gaia close behind.

"It's C4," Oliver said, shining a tiny flashlight up toward the top of the door. "It's wired from the wall down to the doorknob. He moves, it blows."

Jake's knees wobbled dangerously and he pressed his eyes closed. He'd seen enough spy movies in his lifetime to know that C4 was a seriously nasty explosive. Visions of his body being flung across the room, of a giant fireball exploding out the side of the building, of Gaia's limp, dead form, flashed across his mind's eye.

Oh, no. He really *was* going to pee in his pants.

"How much?" Tom asked.

"Enough to take off the top of this building," Oliver said. "But it's a rudimentary device. Not a problem."

Jake liked the sound of that. He opened his eyes and saw Oliver pull a pair of clippers out of his utility belt. Then he reached up with the flashlight toward Jake.

"What?" Jake asked.

"You'll need to hold this with your other hand so I can see what I'm doing," Oliver said.

The beads of sweat along Jake's hairline organized themselves into one large rivulet and danced right down the center of his nose. He was sweating, he was shaking, and he wasn't sure how much longer he could hold on to the doorknob, let alone the flashlight. He looked down at Oliver helplessly, feeling like the useless wuss he clearly was.

"You can do it, Jake," Gaia said in his ear, her voice firm and full of confidence. It was also completely devoid of fear. Apparently when she knew she was about to be blown to bits she didn't let it bother her.

Jake nodded slowly. He grasped the flashlight in his sweaty fingers. Oliver guided Jake's hand until the light was pointing where he needed it to be. Jake's heart hammered in his ears and he found himself silently praying—something he hadn't done once since his mother died. He'd kind of had a problem with God since then.

Oliver cut the casing off the red wire and looked at the circuits inside. Then he did the same to the green wire, and the blue. Jake held his breath. If this was such a rudimentary device, then what the heck was taking so long?

"Got it," Oliver said, once the circuits inside the yellow wire were exposed.

He placed the wire-cutters around the circuits and Jake waited for his life to flash before his eyes, but it didn't. All he saw was his mother's face, then his father's, then his mother's, then his father's. His dad was going to be really pissed at him if he died and left him all alone.

Then Jake heard the clip and the door swung free of his grasp. He sucked in a breath, still alive.

"See? No problem," Oliver said, holding the door open.

Jake stumbled into the room and fell onto the bed, his knees finally giving out. He felt an overwhelming urge to cry, but the second Gaia stepped into view he squelched it. He'd already proven himself to be enough of a wimp right in front of her face. He wasn't going to be a blubbering baby as well.

"You okay?" Gaia asked, standing in front of him.

"Fine," Jake replied, pressing his hands into the bedspread. "Can't say the same for my ego."

Oliver and Tom headed back out into the living room and Gaia sat down next to Jake, a few inches away. "I should've never asked you to come here," she said.

"You didn't. I volunteered," Jake reminded her, pushing both hands into his hair.

"But I didn't try to stop you," Gaia said. She looked down at her clasped hands between her knees. "That's not like me."

"And it's not like me to stay behind no matter what you say," Jake replied. He took in a long, shaky breath and let it out in a loud burst of air. "But I gotta say, I'm not so sure if I'm cut out for this stuff. Five minutes ago I was James Bond and now I feel like I left my spine somewhere in the living room."

He hung his head, ashamed, the rapid beating of his heart pounding in his ears.

"What, you think you're some kind of loser because you got scared?" Gaia asked.

Jake scoffed. "You have a way with words."

He saw Gaia flush out of the corner of his eye and smiled slightly. "Jake, you wouldn't be *human* if you weren't petrified by what just—"

Gaia abruptly stopped talking and looked away. Her jaw clenched and he could see her fighting something off—something she didn't want to think about. So maybe she was affected by the idea of being blown to bits.

"You're gonna be fine," Gaia said, standing—averting her gaze. "Let's get back to work."

There was something she wasn't telling him—Jake could sense it—but now was not the time to ask. He could hear Oliver and Tom crashing around in the living room, searching. The longer they stayed here, the longer Yuri was out there, free to plot whatever he was plotting. Jake made himself stand up and start moving.

While Gaia searched the closet and dresser, Jake rifled through the drawers in the bedside tables, which were empty except for a few pencils, a pair of glasses, and an old watch. He dropped to the floor and looked under the bed. There was a bunch of random stuff shoved underneath the mattress and he started pulling it out. A sleeping bag, a pair of tall rubber boots. . . and then his hand hit something hard.

Jake's pulse seized up as he yanked it free. It was a laptop and it looked like someone had taken a sledgehammer to it. The screen was mangled and half the keyboard had been smashed to bits, but the hard drive was still inside.

"Check it out," Jake said, standing. He set the

computer on the bed as Gaia crossed the room in two long strides.

"Dad!" she shouted, excited.

Tom and Oliver had entered the room in less than a second. Together they all gathered around the laptop, knowing this could be what they were looking for.

"Where did you find this?" Tom asked.

"Under the bed," Jake said. "Look—whoever destroyed this thing wasn't paying much attention—the hard drive is still intact."

"So it is," Oliver said, picking up the computer and inspecting it. "Which means we should be able to extract whatever is on it."

"Good job," Tom said, clapping Jake on the back.

Gaia smiled and Jake felt himself relaxing—grinning even. Suddenly all his fear and shame were washed away, replaced by the pride of accomplishment.

"See?" Gaia said. "You're fine."

"It's a roller-coaster ride, kid," Oliver said with a small smile. "But you'll get used to it."

He thinks I'm good, Jake realized. *He thinks I can do this for real.*

Tom clapped his shoulder again and Jake followed the others out of the room, practically glowing. Oliver was right. Excitement followed by dread, followed by sickening shame, followed by elation and pride. It was a roller coaster. And Jake could definitely get used to the ride.

GAIA AWOKE TO THE SMELL OF

frying bacon and was sure she was still dreaming. Breakfast was usually courtesy of Dunkin' Donuts, Krispy Kreme, or, every now and again, McDonald's. She **Bliss** couldn't remember the last time breakfast had actually been made in this apartment. If ever.

A city bus squealed to a stop somewhere on the street below and it knocked Gaia out of her groggy state. She sat up, everything suddenly rushing back to her—the storming of Dmitri's. . . no, *Yuri's* apartment in the wee hours of the morning. The argument she'd had with her father over her going to bed (she wanted to stay up, he insisted she get some rest). Gaia whirled around to look at the digital clock. It was 10:07. She flung the covers aside and headed for the kitchen.

"Morning!" Oliver said from the head of the dining room table.

He was sipping a cup of coffee and tapping away at a computer keyboard. Before Gaia had reluctantly hit the hay, he'd linked Yuri's smashed hard drive to Tom's PC to see if he could get something out of it.

"Anything?" Gaia asked, yawning hugely.

"I'm getting there," Oliver replied.

"Gaia! Want eggs?" her father asked, appearing at the window between the living room/dining room and the kitchen. Gaia's stomach grumbled loud enough for him to hear. Oliver and Tom both chuckled.

"I'll take that as a yes," her father said, disappearing again.

Gaia walked over to the doorway to the kitchen, her bare feet slapping against the hardwood floor. She was about to lambaste her father for letting her sleep so long, but when she opened her mouth, nothing came out. Seeing her father, standing there at the stove, pushing eggs around with a spatula, she was suddenly overwhelmed.

This was it. This was the moment she'd been waiting for for over a year. It was a regular Sunday morning. She was still in her pajamas, her father was making breakfast in a pair of jeans and a worn-in sweater. This was `normalcy.`

"I made them dry, just how you like 'em," her father said, turning around with the frying pan in his hand. He took one look at Gaia and paused. "You okay?"

"I. . ."

She had no idea what to say. Part of her wanted to grab her father and hold on to him, partially to make sure this was really happening and partially to make sure he wouldn't get away again. But that was far too melodramatic. So instead she just stood there, wringing the hem of her oversized T-shirt between her hands.

Gaia's father's face softened. He walked over to her, leaned down, and planted a kiss in the middle of her forehead. Gaia, in that moment, felt bliss.

"I know," he said with a smile. Gaia smiled back. He did know.

"I've got something!" Oliver called from the dining room.

Gaia forgot about breakfast and rushed back to the table. Tom dropped the frying pan back onto the stove and followed. They took position behind Oliver at the computer screen, which was filled with a list of numbers and letters.

"What is it?" Gaia asked.

"It's a list of coordinates, I believe," Oliver said. "Each line seems to have a set of longitude and latitude coordinates embedded into it."

"Cells of the Organization?" Gaia asked, glancing at her father.

"Could be," he replied. "Could be fronts or safe houses. . ."

"Or targets," Oliver said ominously. "We have no way of knowing. And there are hundreds of them. It would be impossible to check all of them out."

Gaia swallowed, a feeling of helplessness settling in over her shoulders. When she'd first heard Oliver's psyched tone, she naively thought he'd figured out exactly where Yuri was, but it could take months to decipher this list—figure out what it meant and whether it was useful.

168

"So what do we do now?" Gaia asked, looking from her father to Oliver and back again.

Her dad stood up straight and rolled his shoulders back. "I may just have an idea."

So Close

TOM STRODE DOWN THE DIMLY LIT hallway leading to Natasha's glass-fronted cell, feeling more focused than he had in years. He was close—he could feel it. All he needed was one more piece of the puzzle to fall into place and he would have Yuri. The nightmare would be over, once and for all.

Now he just had to convince Natasha to give him that last piece, to show him how it all came together.

Tom paused in front of the transparent wall and watched Natasha rise from her cot and approach the glass. A line of tiny holes ran across the front, right at mouth level, so conversations could be had through the bulletproof substance. Tom pulled the list of coordinates and other random numbers out of his breast pocket and slapped it up against the glass, the printout facing the prisoner. For a moment, neither of them moved.

"What does it mean?" Tom asked, his glare boring

into Natasha as he pressed the paper into the glass with his palm.

Her eyes moved back and forth quickly over the page in front of her and he could practically see the gears in her brain working. She knew what the gibberish meant, that much was clear. What she was undecided on was what to do with that knowledge.

"What does it mean, Natasha?" Tom repeated. Her eyes flicked to him as if she was surprised by the sudden interruption in her thought process. "Intel is going to figure it out eventually. You may as well tell me now."

We're so close, he thought, trying to keep his expression impassive. *So. . . close.*

Natasha's mouth curled into her trademark smirk. "I will give you no more help," she said. "You have yet to release my daughter."

"That's because the intel you gave us last time didn't get us anywhere. You know how it works, Natasha. You lead us to an arrest and then we make good on the agreement," Tom told her. "You give me this. . . you help me bring in Yuri, and Tatiana goes free."

"How stupid do you think I am, Tom?" Natasha snapped, her eyes flashing. "You can keep us both here for the rest of our lives dangling my daughter's freedom in front of me whenever you want something. No." She turned her back on him and paced away. "I will give you nothing more. You have betrayed my trust."

Tom saw red and it was all he could do to keep from pounding his fists against the glass. *He* had betrayed *her* trust? Who had wheedled her way into his life? Into his *heart?* And then tried to kill his daughter, for God's sake!

"You know what this is, don't you?" Tom said, the paper fluttering slightly in his hand. "You could help me if you wanted to."

Natasha turned her defiant profile to him and he knew he was right. He knew that somewhere in her mind was the information that he needed—the information that would ensure Gaia's safety. And she was denying him.

"I could have helped you," Tom told her through his teeth. He wondered if the human body could actually shake apart from repressed rage. "I could have gotten you both out of here. You've just sealed your own fate. And your daughter's."

Then he turned on his heel and rushed back down the hallway. The MP at the end of the hall unlocked the door for him and Tom strode through. All he could think, over and over, was that he had failed. Natasha was their last hope for tracking down Yuri, but so far he had failed to get her to talk. And time is of the essence.

If anything happened to Gaia now, it was all on him.

SAM WOKE UP LATE SUNDAY MORNING

to the sound of his cell phone singing the theme from *Star Wars*. He pressed his fingertips into his eyes, then fumbled on the floor for the jacket he'd been wearing last night. The number displayed on the screen was unfamiliar and started with an area code he'd never even seen before. Confused and half asleep, he hit the talk button and brought the phone to his ear.

"Yeah?" he said gruffly, falling back into his pillows.

"Sam? It's Dmitri."

Instantly Sam was awake, heart hammering, senses on the alert, sitting up straight in bed. *He's a very dangerous man,* Gaia's voice said in the back of his mind. *Find out where he is.*

"Oh. . . hey," Sam said, because he had to say something. He bunched his sheet up in his lap and clasped it against his chest, praying for the right things to say. He couldn't mess this up. Gaia needed him.

"I had to leave again," Dmitri told him. "Have you been to the apartment?"

"Yeah. . . I was there yesterday," Sam said, his brain working overtime to choose his words carefully. "Is everything okay?"

"Yes, everything is fine, but I need to see you and Gaia," Dmitri told him.

He's a very dangerous man. . . .

But he didn't sound dangerous. He sounded like Dmitri, the kindly old man who had been a victim of Loki's, just like Sam had been.

"Where are you?" Sam blurted. Luckily it was a logical question under the circumstances. If Dmitri wanted to see them he was going to have to tell him where they would meet.

"I can't tell you that right now," Dmitri said. "But I need you to bring Gaia to the art museum in Philadelphia tomorrow afternoon. I will meet you on the steps at exactly two P.M. I'm trusting you to do this, Sam."

"Whoa, whoa, whoa, Dmitri, what the hell is going on?" Sam asked, his courage growing slightly. Anyone would be completely baffled and freaked by this phone call even if he didn't suspect that Dmitri was bad news. "You can't just expect us to go all the way to Philadelphia without giving us a reason."

"It's for your own safety," Dmitri told him calmly. "Sam, we have to trust each other."

Sam took a deep breath against the hammering in his chest. Gaia told him to trust her and now Dmitri was telling him to trust him. There was a point in time recently when Gaia had shown no confidence in him whatsoever—when she'd accused him of trying to kill her and turned her back on him entirely. Meanwhile, Dmitri had never done anything but help him.

Sam had a choice to make. Who was it going to be? **The girl who had broken his heart and stabbed him in the back,** or the man who'd given him a home and money to get back on his feet?

Sam closed his eyes, his stomach clenching. "Okay," he said. "We'll be there."

It is an odd feeling, knowing there is not a soul on Earth you can trust. I thought I knew Tom. I thought that he would make sure that the CIA made good on its promise. They told me that if I talked, they would free my daughter. I talked, yet my daughter is still in prison. Still sequestered from life. Still suffering. I thought I could trust Tom. But then, how can I blame him, after what I have done to him?

I could have told him what those numbers meant. I could have told him exactly where Yuri is. But what is the point? If Tom goes there, he will die. If Gaia goes there, she will be taken. And Yuri will find some way to punish me and possibly Tatiana as well. Yuri is everywhere. He is everything. And betraying him is a grave mistake. I learned that the hard way.

Sooner or later Tom would have deciphered that Yuri was alive. I gave him nothing when I gave him that information. But if Yuri were to find Tom on his doorstep he would know who sent him there and Tatiana and I would pay with our lives.

I have to do what little I can to protect my daughter. My silence is all I have left.

Still, I hope I am wrong. I hope that Tom will find Yuri and bring him to justice. That Tom will prevail. Yuri must pay for what he has done to us. He must pay.

Who knew that **nothing** donning Kevlar could **to** be so **lose** intimate?

GAIA, JAKE, TOM, AND OLIVER SAT around the dining room table on Sunday afternoon, each poring over a separate copy of Yuri's list of coordinates. Maps covered the table. They were marked with red dots in various places, indicating the listed

Choosing Him

locales. The work was hard and tedious and the longer it went on, the more coiled Gaia became. They were never going to get anywhere this way and they knew it. Just figuring out the locations meant nothing unless someone told them the significance of the list.

The advantage was gone. Yuri was out there somewhere and they were never going to find him.

A sudden rap at the door took them all by surprise. Gaia got up and checked through the peephole. Sam stood on the other side of the door, looking around him like a lamb who'd just been tossed into the lion's den.

"Sam? What's wrong?" Gaia asked, ripping the door open.

"He called me," Sam said, holding out his cell phone like it was an explosive device.

Tom was on his feet in an instant. "Who? Yuri?"

"No. Dmitiri," Sam said, walking into the room and taking in the maps, the endless cups of coffee. . . Jake. And then Oliver. Sam took an instinctive step back and Gaia took an instinctive step closer to him to help him feel safe.

"Dmitri and Yuri are the same guy," Jake said, leaning back in his chair. He rested his muscled arm across the top, nonchalantly showing off his brawn.

"Well, who's Yuri?" Sam asked, ignoring Jake and turning away from Oliver.

"My grandfather. It's a really long story," Gaia began.

"Forget that now. He contacted you?" Tom asked, walking over and taking the cell phone from Sam's trembling fingers.

"Uh. . . yeah. . . it's the last number in there," Sam said, visibly fighting to control his emotions. He stuffed his hands under his arms and pressed his elbows down into his sides. "He wanted me to bring Gaia to meet him. He said two o'clock tomorrow afternoon on the steps at the Philadelphia Museum of Art."

"Philadelphia?" Oliver said, looking over Tom's shoulder as he scrolled to the phone number. Both brothers' faces lit up when they saw the digits displayed there.

"We've got him," Tom said, meeting Oliver's gaze. Gaia's heart took a leap as her uncle looked up at her and smiled. After all this work, after being stonewalled by Natasha, after hours of brainstorming, Sam had just walked in and given them the key.

"How could he be so careless?" Tom asked. "All we

179

have to do is trace this number through the satellite provider and we have his exact location."

"He wants Gaia and he's getting desperate," Oliver said. "Kidnapping her didn't work so he went to his next best hope."

He looked at Sam as he said this and Sam's face went ashen. Gaia had to get him out of there before he got sick or worse. She opened the door and pulled Sam out into the hallway.

"Are you okay?" she asked him.

"This is all a little weird," Sam admitted with an embarrassed laugh. "Dmitri is your grandfather? What the hell is that about? And why is he so dangerous?"

"Sam, my grandfather is a very bad man," Gaia said, looking into Sam's green eyes and feeling more grateful toward him than she'd ever felt toward anyone. "And you just helped us find him. We're going to get him because of you."

Sam swallowed and looked down at his shoes. "Gaia, I. . . I don't even know what to say. I'm. . . glad I could help?" he added with a shrug.

"I'm going to explain all of this to you, I swear," Gaia said. "But right now I've got to get back in there and help them."

Sam nodded. "Is there anything else I can do?" He sounded almost hopeful that she'd ask for more. But he'd done enough. And now all she wanted was for him to be safe.

"You have no idea how much you've done already," she said. And then, on impulse, she reached up and hugged him, tightening her arms around his neck. Sam held her so close she could feel his heart beating against her chest, matching the quickened pace of her own pulse. When she pulled away and looked into his eyes it was so simple to imagine herself kissing him. Choosing him. Being with him.

But she couldn't. She was moving on. And Sam had to move on, too.

"Thank you," she told him sincerely.

And before he could say anything more, she slipped back into the apartment and closed the door on Sam.

An Actual Girl

GAIA SAT ACROSS FROM JAKE AT THE dining room table early Sunday afternoon, watching him shovel food into his mouth. She couldn't believe how quickly everything had changed. It had taken less than an hour for her father and Oliver to track Yuri's cell phone down to an address in north Philadelphia. Once they'd come up with a game plan, Oliver had run out to the corner deli and bought sandwiches, salads, and fruit to fortify them for the trip. None of them had taken in a normal meal all day and Oliver was of the opinion that they had no chance against Yuri unless they were well fed and focused.

"Enjoying that?" Gaia asked, raising her eyebrows as Jake shoved half a turkey hero into his mouth at once.

"Uh, you're one to talk," he said, eyeing her chest. Gaia looked down to find a big chunk of potato salad stuck to the front of her light blue T-shirt.

Oh, that's attractive, she thought, wiping it up with her finger.

Jake smiled at her, his blue eyes twinkling, and Gaia flushed. Every time she saw Jake, the temperature of whatever room they were in seemed to skyrocket. More and more she found herself blushing around him. And smiling. And wondering what her hair was doing. She found herself acting like an actual girl.

"Gaia, you have your battle gear?" Tom asked, walking in from his bedroom.

A girl with battle gear, Gaia reminded herself. Somehow she had a feeling she would never qualify for a femininity award.

"Yeah," she said, wiping her mouth with the back

182

of her hand. She grabbed her bulletproof vest from the chair next to her and pulled it on and zipped up the sides. She reached over her left shoulder and groped for the nylon strap, but couldn't get it in her grasp.

"I got it," Jake said, rising from his seat. Gaia couldn't help noticing he used an actual napkin to wipe his face. He came up behind Gaia and lifted the strap. Gaia could feel his breath on her neck and tried not to react, but there was nothing she could do to control the omnipresent tingle.

Sam may have made her pulse race earlier that day, but Jake excited something new inside of her—something she felt in every inch of her body, heart and soul. There was no point in denying it anymore. She was falling for him.

"You okay?" Jake asked, as he snapped the strap to her shoulder and tightened it.

Gaia swallowed hard, her throat constricting. Who knew that donning Kevlar could be so intimate?

"Fine," Gaia replied. She went over to the table and picked up the paper plates and bags and soda cans. "You better get ready."

Her arms full, Gaia kicked open the kitchen door and dumped everything into the trash. She paused in front of the sink to catch her breath and get her pounding heart under control. Through the kitchen window she could see Oliver, Jake, and her father talking in low tones, going over the game plan as Jake secured his protective gear.

Aside from the vibe of attraction constantly sizzling between her and Jake, there was also an air of determination in the room that affected everyone, not least of all Gaia. This was it. By the end of the day today, it would all be over. She would be free.

Life as she knew it was about to change. For the better. For good.

Gaia took a deep breath and Jake tore his attention away from the elder men, looking over at her. Their eyes met and Gaia froze. As if in slow motion, Jake's eyes softened and he smiled a slight, private smile. It turned Gaia's insides to goo and she had the sudden, almost overwhelming desire to rush right out there, grab him, and kiss him.

Jake's smile widened as if he knew what she was thinking, and Gaia forced herself to look away, `closing the little shutters over the opening`. She turned around and leaned back against the sink, her hands braced against the counter, her elbows behind her.

Gaia did want to kiss him. More than anything. And she would. Later. After it was over. When they were both safe and sound and victorious.

She would kiss Jake Montone as soon as she had nothing to lose.

"IF ANYTHING GOES WRONG AND

Grandpa

you can't speak into your hand-held, just press this button," Gaia's father explained, holding up his tiny walkie-talkie. "You press this button on the side and the rest of us will be able to track you anywhere within a ten-mile radius."

Gaia nodded her understanding. Every order, every instruction her father had given that afternoon had been repeated in layman's terms again and again as if he thought he were speaking to a group of kindergartners. She knew he just wanted them to be prepared, but enough was enough. Gaia was more than ready to go.

She looked out past the bushes that concealed her, Jake, Oliver, and Tom, gazing across the wide lawn at the mansion hulking against the twilit sky. At least a quarter mile of open green grass separated the little team from the target. If Yuri had any guards stationed outside, which was an obvious no-brainer, they would spot Gaia and the others before they made it five feet from the brush.

She considered mentioning this, but she was sure her father, Oliver and Jake were all well aware of the situation. Unfortunately, there was nothing they could do about it. This was the best route onto the grounds unless they wanted to walk en masse up the driveway out front.

"Remember, we want to head for the basement. If he's got a panic room, that's where it'll be," Tom added.

Come on. Enough instruction, Gaia thought, her leg jittering beneath her. *Let's get this over with already.*

"This Yuri guy sure knows how to live," Jake said, scanning the back of the huge house.

"That's all about to change," Tom told him. "Okay, Jake and Oliver take the west side, Gaia and I will go east."

Everyone nodded and a thrill of excitement rushed through Gaia. This was it. If they succeeded here today, life as she knew it was over. How totally cool.

"Move out," Tom said.

Gaia cast Jake what she hoped was an encouraging look before following her father through the woods toward the right side of the house. Every twig and leaf that crunched beneath their feet sounded loud enough to wake the dead. Gaia kept one eye trained on the house, but there was no sign of life. So far, so good.

Her father suddenly paused beside a huge oak and pressed himself back against the trunk. He motioned to Gaia to stay down, but over the top of the brush Gaia could see what had stopped him. A single gun-toting guard moved from around the side of the house to the back, patrolling along the perimeter.

"That's not too obvious," Gaia said sarcastically.

"He has his back turned," her father said flatly. "Stay low."

He rushed out of the bushes, legs bent, back down, moving quickly across the lawn. Gaia followed him, wondering if he was scared, if he was worried that they might not pull this off. It was one rare moment in her life that she was actually grateful she was a freak who couldn't feel fear. Yuri seemed like the type of character who could inspire terror in anyone. It was still so hard to imagine Dmitri as a psychopath.

They made it to the wall with no incident and sat back against it, taking shallow breaths. Gaia trained her ears toward the other side of the house, listening for anything out of the ordinary, but was met with silence. Wherever Jake and Oliver were, they were okay. So far.

"I'll check the window," Gaia's father told her. He stood up and ran a circuitry detector along the bottom of the window above Gaia's head. The green light blinked rapidly and Tom attached it to the glass. He pressed a button, then crouched down again.

"What's that do?" Gaia asked.

There was a sizzle and a pop from above them and her father stood up and opened the window. No alarm.

"It shorts out all the wiring in the vicinity," he explained, motioning for her to climb inside. "Let's go."

Impressed, Gaia swung her leg over the window and lowered herself into a vacant room. No furniture, no artwork, no light fixtures. Everything was still.

"Looks like we picked the right room," Gaia whispered when her father appeared beside her.

He nodded tersely and headed for the door. Gaia pressed her lips together and told herself to remember why they were here. Her father had a reason for being all business. This was a huge mission and if he wanted her to keep her mouth shut—as he seemed to be telling her by his own example—she would do just that.

Her father checked outside the door, then motioned to her to follow. They speed-walked along the wall down a long corridor that appeared to open up onto a large room. The hallway split at one point, but her father stayed the course—heading for the front of the house. Suddenly Gaia heard male voices up ahead and she and her father both froze. He looked around the corner and pulled his head back.

"Two guards, playing poker," he whispered to her. "Stay here."

Gaia resisted the urge to protest. Why was she always staying behind him, staying low, staying back? Didn't he trust her to hold her own—to help more?

Her dad stepped out of the hallway, dart gun drawn, and fired. There was a commotion and a gun went off. Gaia's father ducked back into the hallway and a piece of the wall across from them exploded.

"There are two more," he told Gaia as the shots and shouts intensified. "They walked in from the other room." He reloaded his dart gun and looked her in the eye. "I'm gonna hold them here. You go back to that fork in the hallway and see if you can find a way to the basement."

Gaia's heart thumped as he `jumped into the fray` again and fired a few more shots from his dart gun.

"Why are you still here?" he hissed when he ducked back again.

"I'm not leaving you here with three guards," she told him, pulling out her own dart gun.

"Yes you are." He grabbed her arm and nudged her back in the direction they'd come from. "Go!"

Gaia hesitated.

"We're here for Yuri, Gaia," he said fiercely. "I know you can take him. I'll be right behind you."

That was all she needed to hear. Gaia drew herself up straight and ran double time back down the hallway, buoyed by her father's confidence. Every door along the new hall led to another unused salon or bedroom, but at the very end of the hall, Gaia found a reinforced steel door—quite unlike the standard wood doors she'd already tried.

This looks promising, she thought.

She turned the knob, but it was locked. Gaia had a

loaded gun in an ankle holster, but she had been instructed not to use it unless absolutely necessary. Besides, she didn't want to draw attention to herself by blasting the lock to smithereens. Instead she crouched to the floor and pulled out a lock-picking pin and fork from her utility belt. She hadn't practiced this particular skill since she was in grade school and Loki had secretly trained her behind her parents' backs, but even then she was an expert.

Gaia inserted the tools into the lock, trying not to pay attention to the continued gunshots in another area of the house. She had to focus. Her father would be with her any minute.

Suddenly the mechanism inside the doorknob clicked and Gaia's pulse jumped. "Like riding a bike," she whispered.

She tried the knob and held her breath as it turned. Standing, Gaia opened the door ever so slowly, waiting for more gunfire, an order to stand down— something. But the door swung open and Gaia stood there, looking down a darkened set of stairs.

Bingo, she thought, replacing her tools in her belt. She drew out the dart gun again and started down the steps, walking as lightly as humanly possible. The stairs grew narrower toward the bottom and ended at a wall. The only direction Gaia could go was left. She pressed herself back against the wall and checked around the corner.

One guard stood before another metal door at the base of another set of stairs coming in from the right. He spoke rapidly into a wrist mike while more voices crackled through the speaker in his ear, so loud Gaia could hear the distortion all the way down the hall.

"I need a guard at the back door!" the man said into his mike. "Someone secure the back basement door."

At that moment, he looked up and saw Gaia emerging from the stairs.

"Too late," she said with a shrug. `Before he could even pull his gun out, she had flattened him with a dart to the chest.` Then Gaia raced down the hallway, her adrenaline pumping at a fierce rate.

This door was secured with an electric keypad lock. There was a keycard slot down the side. Gaia crouched to the ground and flipped the comatose guard over. She searched his pockets and found a card with a metallic strip attached by a metal wire to his belt. She yanked as hard as she could and the wire snapped.

"Let this work," Gaia said under her breath.

She checked over her shoulder for her father or for the guard her downed-man had ordered, but saw nothing. Pulling her gun out for good measure, Gaia stood and slipped the card through the lock box. The red light on the side turned green and a loud clang emitted from the doorway.

Gaia stepped back, held her gun up with both hands, and kicked the door with all her might. It flew open, slamming back against the wall, and Gaia trained her gun straight ahead.

"Don't move!" a voice shouted.

Yuri stood on the other side of a richly decorated room near yet another, even thicker, door. He had a gun `trained on Gaia's head.` His eyes widened ever so slightly when he saw her.

"I said, don't move!" he told her again.

"You're not going to shoot me," Gaia said.

She reached back with her foot and slammed the door behind her. Any of the guards would have key-cards as well, but the closed door would buy her a few extra seconds if they did come.

"What makes you think that?" Yuri asked as she sidestepped into the room, her gun pointed right at his face. He followed her with his own weapon, circling around a leather couch to stay across from her.

"Because, I'm your only hope now, right? I'm supposed to be groomed to succeed you, aren't I, *Yuri*?" She paused and ground her teeth together. `"Or should I call you Grandpa?"` she asked with a sneer.

"Do you think I'm going to let *you* kill *me*?" he asked.

"Not planning on it," Gaia said. "I'd rather see you rot in a federal prison for the rest of your life."

Yuri chuckled. He ran one hand along his freshly

shaven jaw line and smiled at her. "You can't turn me in," he told her. "I have video of you stealing files from a CIA office. If I go down, granddaughter, so do you."

Granddaughter. Somehow, the word lost its warm and fuzzy feel when spoken by a man pointing a deadly weapon at her face.

Gaia felt sick, but she didn't let it show. He may have been her grandfather, but he was clearly still the enemy.

"Are you actually trying to *threaten* me?" she asked, her elbows locked. "I thought you were supposed to be some kind of sociopathic genius, but you're just another idiot if you think that that matters to me."

Yuri continued to smile, his eyes glittering. "Careful, now. My sociopathic idiot blood is running through your veins."

Gaia swallowed back the bile that instantly appeared in her throat. She didn't have an answer for that.

"Just think about it, Gaia," Yuri said, seeing an opening. "If you join me I can help you reach your full potential in a way your father never can. He's holding you back. He doesn't want you to know what you're capable of, but I do. Gaia, I want the world for you. . . ."

He lowered his gun and started to pace at a safe distance, relaxing as he talked. Gaia followed him with her gun by her arms, which were starting to shake, by her vision, beginning to blur with tears. Frustrated that he seemed so calm. He didn't think she would shoot him. He didn't think she had it in her.

"It's what your mother would have wanted, Gaia," he said, pausing and turning to look into her eyes. "I'm your grandfather. Don't you think Katia would have wanted us to be together?"

"She hated you," Gaia spat, one tear brimming over. "She fled her country because of you. If she were here right now, she'd tell me to kill you."

Yuri paled slightly and in that moment Gaia felt truly murderous for the first time in her life. She had never killed anyone in cold blood. She'd never even punched someone who hadn't attacked her first. But right then, she knew she could do it. She could take this evil bastard out right then and probably even feel good about it. No guilt. No remorse.

But he is your grandfather, a little voice in Gaia's mind told her. *He could tell you things about yourself. . . your history. Things you may otherwise never know.*

Gaia was too close to this. She had to get control of herself. Hand trembling, she reached down to her belt and hit the button on the side of her mini-walkie-talkie.

"What are you doing?" Yuri asked, brandishing his weapon again and taking a few steps toward her.

Gaia fired a warning shot over his shoulder, taking out a few books on a shelf behind him. Yuri froze.

"I missed on purpose," she told him. "Move again and you're worm food."

Yuri swallowed hard and eyed her gun. Gaia only hoped someone would come and relieve her before she used it again.

TOM STALKED ALONG THE PERIMETER

Time to Die

of the house, doubling back to the window he and Gaia had come through the first time. During the firefight he'd managed to subdue four guards, but the chaos had taken him outside. He needed to retrace his steps so he could find the hallway he'd sent Gaia through.

How could I have let her go alone? Tom berated himself, struggling to catch his breath, racing more from nerves than exertion. *Yes, she's capable, but she's your daughter, idiot.*

Suddenly the red light on his GPS receiver started to blink and Tom whipped it free from his belt. Gaia had hit her panic button, but the information on the digital tracking screen couldn't have been right. According to the dots on the display that represented his location and Gaia's, she was right on top of him.

Or beneath *me,* Tom realized, his heart seizing up.

He looked down and spotted a long, low window near his feet. Tom dropped to the ground and peered through the glass. There, just below him, was Yuri himself. And he was pointing a gun at Gaia's face.

Tom's paternal instinct didn't even register the fact that Gaia also had a weapon trained on Yuri. All he knew was that he had to get in there and help her. He had to get in there now.

Flipping over onto his back, Tom turned around so that his feet were facing the glass. He said a quick prayer, pulled his legs back, and thrust them forward, shattering the glass. A cacophony of alarms sounded out across the grounds. Tom squirmed through the window, landed hard on his feet, and tumbled right into Yuri, taking him down in a pile of limbs.

Yuri's knee came down on Tom's forearm and he heard the snap before he felt the intense shot of pain. He shouted out, a primal growl, and struggled to free himself, but it was no use. Yuri may have been old, but he was still powerful. Without his right arm, Tom couldn't win.

"Get off him!" Gaia shouted with all of her energy.

"Gaia, don't!" Tom shouted, knowing that if she joined the scrum she would be disarmed.

Suddenly he felt an arm around his neck and was hauled to his feet. Just then the door behind Gaia burst open and Jake and Oliver rushed in, guns at the ready. They flanked Gaia and all three watched in grim surprise as Yuri grasped Tom to him and pressed the barrel of his gun to Tom's temple.

"Dad!" Gaia shouted helplessly, her gun still drawn.

Tom tried to speak, but Yuri's grip choked him.

"I want all of you to see this," Yuri said.

From the corner of his eye, Tom could see that Yuri held something in his right hand—the hand that was free while his forearm pressed into Tom's larynx. It looked like some kind of remote control, but Tom couldn't be sure.

"Tom and I are going to be leaving here together and if any one of you tries to stop us I will shoot him, then blow this entire place."

Gaia's gaze flicked to Tom. He knew his own eyes were filled with fear and he wished for a moment that he had Gaia's power—that he could show his daughter a pair of clear, undisturbed eyes—but he couldn't. He didn't care about himself, but he didn't want her to die. And it seemed like Yuri was more than willing to make that happen.

This is it, Tom thought, looking at his brother with grim resignation. Looking at the three guns pointed at himself and his captor. *It's time for me to die. And either Jake, Oliver, or Gaia is going to have to kill me.*

I realized something about myself today. I realized that I love Gaia Moore. Not just love her like, "Oh, yeah, love you, too." But I love her with every ounce of my soul. I love her more than I've ever loved anyone before. In fact, I don't think I ever *have* loved anyone before, because this feels totally different than what I had with Heather last year or with Anna back in high school. This feels real. This feels more than real. It feels. . . transcendent.

There's nothing I won't do for her. That's what brought this realization home. If I can choose her over a man who has been nothing but a friend to me. If I can put her safety before my own. If I can stand in the very same room with the person who snatched me away from my life, my family, my friends for months and not go insane. If I can do all of that for her, then it must be love.

I told her that I'll meet with

her uncle and I will. I'll do that and anything else she asks of me. Anything to prove my love to her. Because she loves me, too. I can see it in her eyes. This Jake guy seems like he's in right now. Like he's involved in whatever's going on with Dmitri or Yuri or whoever the hell he is. But that doesn't matter. Jake is too new. Too green. He can't possibly know Gaia as well as I do. Gaia and I have a history—a whole heart-wrenching, mutual lust and longing kind of history. And that doesn't just go away because some mojo-having tool enters the picture.

No. Gaia loves me. It may be buried. It may be confused with something else. It may be a while before she realizes it. But Gaia Moore is mine. We were meant to be together. We're soul mates.

And sooner or later she's going to realize it, too.

She'd done plenty of stupid things in her **peaceful** life, but now **silence** was not the time to add to the idiocy list.

The Idiocy List

"KILL HIM!" TOM GROWLED, HIS throat constricting in pain, his voice sounding like something otherworldly. "Open fire! Kill the bastard!"

Gaia gripped her gun with all her might, feeling as if it was the only thing in the room over which she had any control. The touch of the cool steel against her hand grounded her—helped her focus. She knew what her father was really saying. He wanted them to take them both out—Yuri *and* her father if necessary—just to take Yuri down.

Sorry, Dad. Not gonna happen, Gaia thought, staring into his eyes. She wasn't about to lose her father now. Not when they were so close to being a family again. Not when they were close enough to taste their own freedom.

"I know you won't do anything stupid, granddaughter," Yuri said, his glare boring into her skull as if he could read her thoughts.

Well then, you obviously don't know me that well, Gaia thought. She'd done plenty of stupid things in her life, but now was not the time to add to the idiocy list.

Gaia assessed the situation before her, the seconds dragging away like hours. As far as she could tell, she had one option. It wasn't a clear shot, but if her aim was true, it would work.

201

She looked at Oliver. *I'm making my move,* she thought, hoping she somehow conveyed that message in her face. Then she gave Jake the same look, lifting her chin ever so slightly to tell him where to go. If Oliver dove right he should be able to take cover behind the leather couch. If Jake dove left, he could duck and roll behind a wooden credenza. It wouldn't give him much protection, but it was something.

Jake narrowed his eyes slightly and Gaia knew he understood her.

She turned her head, closed one eye, and took aim. The last thing she saw before the bullet left the chamber was Yuri's mouth opening in surprise.

Jake and Oliver leapt for cover as the bullet grazed the shoulder of Tom's already maimed arm and embedded directly into Yuri's. Both men tumbled backward and the detonator flew from Yuri's grasp, skittering across the floor and coming to rest right in front of the sofa behind which Oliver now crouched.

Yuri fired into the air as he fell, but his ammo hit nothing but wall, ceiling, and bookcase. Tom gained his balance and dug his knee into Yuri's shattered shoulder. A gut-wrenching cry ripped through the room, but Tom didn't hesitate. He grabbed Yuri's gun with his left hand and stood, his broken right arm held protectively against his chest, blood oozing from the wound on his shoulder.

Gaia stepped up next to her father and pointed her own gun down at Yuri as well. Jake soon joined them. Oliver dismantled the detonator, then trained a fourth weapon on their mark.

Broken and defeated, Yuri lay on his back on the floor, sirens screaming through the night. Gaia saw him glance toward the door where three guards now lay, sleeping soundly.

There's no one left to save you, Gaia thought, gazing at him coldly. He seemed to realize this at the same moment, closed his eyes, and laid his head back on the floor.

"It's over," Gaia's father said.

Gaia looked at him and smiled. "It's over."

GAIA AND JAKE WALKED DOWN THE

Sweet Relief

winding driveway behind Oliver and Yuri, who shuffled along, his feet and hands shackled. Small electric lights lined the drive, casting a soft glow over the area. The rumble of an engine split the air and all four of them paused as a pair of headlights swung into view. A moment later, the black van Oliver had procured for their road trip came around a bend in the driveway.

Tom was in the driver's seat, one hand on the wheel, the other taped against him in a makeshift sling.

The brakes squeaked as he brought the van to a stop a few yards ahead of them. Tom got out of the car and went about helping Oliver lift Yuri into the back of the van. The moment all three men disappeared behind the vehicle, Gaia felt a thrill run through her.

This was it. This was her moment.

She looked at Jake. He gazed back at her. About a thousand crickets chirped in the darkness around them, but aside from their song and the quietly idling engine, there was nothing but peace. `Peaceful silence outside. Peaceful silence in Gaia's heart.`

It was over. And that morning she had made herself a promise. If they came through this alive and well, there was something she was going to do.

Gaia took a step closer to Jake and she saw the question in his eyes just before she wrapped her hand around his neck, pulled him to her, and kissed him like she'd never kissed anybody before. There was no hesitation. No uncertainty. No concern for what he thought, what anyone else would think. Gaia knew what she wanted and for once in her screwed-up life, she felt free to take it.

Jake wrapped his arms around her back and lifted her until she was standing on her toes. He had a confident, strong kiss. Not sloppy or overeager or unsure.

His touch sent chills up and down Gaia's back and through her heart. It cleared her mind of everything except him. His lips on hers, his fingers in her hair, his arms clutching her to him.

It was more than perfect. It was surreal. And when they heard the van doors slam, they pulled their faces away from each other, but never let go completely. Gaia looked up into Jake's clear blue eyes as her mind slowly started to function again. Jake closed his eyes and touched his forehead to hers, letting out a sigh that sounded like sweet relief.

This is where it all begins, Gaia thought, a fluttering of happiness tickling her heart. *Out with the old life, in with the new.*

TOM TOOK HIS SEAT AT THE GLEAMING

Taking Lumps

black table in the debriefing room, as if he were about to face a firing squad. His sore arm throbbed within its cast for the first time all morning as if it sympathized with his plight. There had been no doubt in Tom's mind when he'd taken off to find Yuri on his own that he would meet with dissent upon his return. But he had hoped that the success of his mission—the fact that he'd just turned over one of the world's most wanted criminals—would deflect the ire of his superiors somewhat. From the level of tension in the room, however, it appeared that this was not the case.

Director Vance sat directly across from Tom, flanked by Agent Frenz and Agent Jack Freelander from Internal Affairs. Their expressions were grim except for Agent Frenz, who seemed to be smirking without moving one muscle in his face.

"Well, Agent Moore, what have you got to say for yourself?" Director Vance said, lacing his fingers together on the table, his shoulders hunched forward. Even with bad posture the man was intimidating.

"You're welcome?" Tom asked archly.

Freelander laughed but quickly covered his mouth with his fist and disguised it as a cough. With his good arm, Tom nonchalantly reached for the clear pitcher of water on the table and poured out a glass for the man, then slid it across the table toward him.

"I'd advise you that being flip will get you nowhere," Vance said. "I believe I told you not to go off on your own."

Tom sighed. If Vance had really wanted to prevent Tom from his mission, he could have stopped him. He could have had him detained at the door for disobeying a direct order. But the fact was that Vance had always known Tom was their best shot for bringing down Yuri. He had let the whole Philadelphia mission happen by not doing enough to stop Tom. That meant they had both gone against procedure. Unfortunately, it wouldn't look like that to any IA committee because Vance had covered his ass by ordering Tom to lay off.

Tom had brought down a highly dangerous international terrorist and he was going to get no credit. Instead he was going to be reprimanded. He knew this and had accepted it, but that didn't mean he was going to just sit here and take his lumps quietly.

"Am I suspended or not?" Tom asked, leaning back in his chair. His shoulder twinged and he managed, somehow, not to wince.

Vance took a deep breath and looked at Freelander. The smaller man took a sip of his water and placed the glass down on the table.

"Under normal circumstances a suspension would be in order, but these are not normal circumstances," he said. "The internal affairs committee has reviewed your reports and the statements of several agents and has determined that it would be against this country's interests to deactivate you at this juncture."

Tom held his breath, uncertain if he should allow himself to believe what he'd just heard.

"What?" Frenz blurted, leaning forward to see Freelander past Vance's sizable frame. "How is he not suspended?"

"Agent Frenz," Vance snapped, holding up a hand. Frenz sat back in his seat, petulant. Tom tried not to smile. "Agent Moore, you will be taking the rest of the week off, however, and this time I will not be calling you to come back in. I suggest you take these few days to relax, spend some time with your daughter, and not do anything stupid."

"You can count on it, sir," Tom said, letting the grin break through.

He stood slowly as Frenz and Freelander exited the room. He flinched in surprise when Vance extended his arm across the table. There was a split second of hesitation before Tom lifted his left hand and shook with his superior.

"Good work, Moore," Vance said.

"Thank you, sir," Tom replied.

Vance pulled his hand back and straightened his suit jacket. "I never said that," he warned.

"Of course not, sir."

"We'll see you next week," Vance told him, holding the door open for Tom.

"Yes you will," Tom replied. As he slid by Vance, turning sideways instinctively to protect his broken arm, Tom lifted his chin. In the end, the meeting had gone better than he'd imagined. And now he had a few days off to do with them what he wanted. He didn't even have to think twice to know what that was.

"*Spend some time with your daughter,*" he thought, recalling Vance's words as he headed for the nearest exit. *I like the sound of that.*

WHAT THE HELL AM I DOING HERE?

Repentance

Sam wondered, pressing his back up against the armrest on the wooden bench in Prospect Park as he watched Oliver approach. The moment Sam laid eyes on the man his throat filled with bile and his veins with hatred and fear. He had chosen the park because it was a public place—always crowded on spring days like this one with joggers and stroller-pushing mothers and cops on horseback. But even with the dozens of people milling around within a hundred-yard radius, Sam suddenly felt alone. Utterly alone—just like he had for those months he'd spent in this bastard's excuse for a prison.

"Sam," Oliver said, stopping next to the bench. He wore a new-looking black trench coat over gray pants and a white shirt. His expression was unreadable, his eyes soft.

God, I hope he doesn't try to squeeze out a few tears, Sam thought, fighting against the sickness in his throat. *Why did I ever say I would do this?*

"Gaia and I are both grateful that you agreed to meet me."

Right. Because of Gaia.

"Let's get this over with," Sam told him, gratefully spotting a uniformed police officer at the far end of the winding path their bench fronted. "Say what you've got to say."

Oliver tucked his coat under himself and sat down next to Sam. If there were any way to move farther away from the psycho, Sam would have. But as it was, he was trapped. All he could do was hope that the apology, or whatever this was, would be short and sweet.

Unfortunately, the silence started to drag. Oliver reached into his pocket and pulled out a large coin—one of those old, rare, fifty-cent pieces—and started to roll it over, end over end, on top of his fingers. Sam stared at the movement of the coin, mesmerized by the agility it took to control it. Then the man's leg started to bounce up and down and Sam snapped out of his momentary trance.

"Look, if you've got nothing to say," he said, starting to get up.

"Sit down!" Oliver snapped, his voice harsh.

A cold, blasting chill shot through Sam. Against his better judgment he fell back onto the bench—mostly because his leg muscles ceased to work the moment the man exploded. That was not the voice of a repentant man. It wasn't even the voice of a man who wanted to *fake* repentance.

Sam swallowed hard. He watched the coin spin faster and faster. Watched the leg twitch spasmodically. From the corner of his eye, he kept a close watch on the cop's position.

"Oliver," he said quietly. "I've. . . never seen anyone do that with a coin before."

Instantly, the coin stopped. It fell flat on top of Oliver's fingers. The man looked down at it as if he'd never seen it before. The leg stopped moving. Oliver's brows knit together. He pocketed the coin and looked up at Sam.

"I hadn't even realized I was doing that," he said apologetically. "Nervous habit, I suppose."

Sam nodded, attempting to keep the shivers that were coursing through him like waves at bay. There was something frightening going on here. He hated to admit it, even to himself, but this man did not seem to be the person Gaia thought he was.

"I've asked you here today to tell you that I am deeply sorry for everything I've done," Oliver said, looking Sam in the eye. "To you, to Gaia, to everyone who had the misfortune of coming into contact with—"

Don't say it. Don't say it, Sam told himself. But he had to. He had to find out if he was right.

"With Loki," he finished.

Immediately, the coin came out again. The flipping resumed. The leg began to twitch. Oliver, Loki, whoever the hell he was, stared out across the park toward the nearby woods, his eyes narrowing into slits.

It's him, Sam thought, the fear like knives to his skull and heart. *He's back. He's coming back.*

"I've got to go," Sam said, standing quickly this time.

"Where, Sam?" the man asked, his voice entirely

different than it had been moments before. He sounded amused—venomously amused. "Where do you think you're going?"

But this time, Sam wasn't stupid enough to pause. He took off in the direction of the police officer even though his apartment was on the opposite end of the park. His instinct was to be as close to as much protection as humanly possible, just in case.

Nothing happened, however. Loki didn't chase him. He didn't try to gun him down. He just let Sam go, his pulse racing the whole way. As soon as Sam reached the edge of the park and acknowledged his good fortune in still being alive, he turned his steps toward the subway, checking over his shoulder every few seconds until he could have given himself whiplash.

I have to warn Gaia, he thought, his pace quickening. *I have to warn her that Loki is back.*

"OLIVER KICKS ASS. I MEAN, literally. That man is the Terminator," Jake said, putting his feet up on the just-delivered wooden cof-  fee table at Gaia's apartment. "You should have seen how quick he took down those two guys at Yuri's. I hope I'm still that good when I'm old."

"Jake?" Gaia said.

"Yeah?" he asked, crooking his arms behind his head as he leaned back.

"You're doing it again. The rambling thing," Gaia told him.

"Sorry. Won't happen again," Jake joked.

As Gaia scooched down into the couch until she was almost at eye level with her feet up next to Jake's, he leaned over and planted a kiss right on her mouth. Gaia's heart did a few million somersaults. Jake slumped back next to her, smiling. If Gaia wasn't so happy she knew the both of them would have been making her sick right now.

"Are we going to watch this movie or what?" Jake asked.

Gaia grabbed the remote and started the DVD player. She'd only agreed to watch Jake's favorite movie, *The Fast and the Furious*, when he'd told her she could crack as many jokes as she wished during the viewing. But even though the choice of film was less than optimal, Gaia couldn't help smiling as the credits started to roll.

This was so normal, vegging on the couch watching a movie on a Tuesday afternoon after school. When, exactly, was she going to wake up from this?

There was a knock on the door and Gaia and Jake exchanged a look.

"Gaia, it's Sam."

Jake rolled his eyes and Gaia jumped up from the couch. She knew that Sam and Oliver were supposed to meet this afternoon and she'd fully expected a rundown phone call from one or both of them later this evening, but a drop-by was a surprise. Gaia glanced through the open kitchen door as she passed it, checking out the microwave clock. It was only 4:45 and they were supposed to be meeting at four. How had Sam gotten here so fast?

"Hey," she said, opening the door. "What's up?"

The two-word question was barely out of her mouth when Sam had passed right by her and into the living room. Gaia let the door slam and followed. Jake pushed himself off the couch and faced Sam as he entered the room.

Great. Just what I needed to puncture the mood, Gaia thought. *A little more macho posturing.*

Jake picked up the remote and paused the already noisy movie. For a moment, Gaia stood behind Sam, uncertain of how to proceed, feeling guilty over interrupting a private moment with another guy. But then she reminded herself that however her heart felt at this moment she'd already made a decision to start over. With Jake. And there was no reason to hide that.

It was her life. Her decision.

She walked around the L-shaped extension of the

couch and joined Jake on the other side, standing next to him.

"You guys remember each other, right?" she said, the words coming out in a speedy jumble.

"Sam, right?" Jake said, crossing his arms over his chest.

"And you're Jake," Sam said. His gaze only rested on the other guy for a second before flicking to Gaia. "Can I talk to you alone?"

Gaia could see that Sam was scared. She gave Jake a guilt-filled glance, then led Sam down the hall toward her room. She paused just outside the door and looked Sam in the eye.

"What happened?" she asked in a whisper.

"Loki is reemerging," Sam told her quietly, his eyes darting toward the living room.

Gaia scoffed. "Not possible."

"Gaia, you know I wouldn't lie to you about this," Sam implored, sounding desperate. "We were sitting in Prospect Park and he kept zoning out. And whenever he did he started twitching and. . . and he was playing with this coin, all methodical. . . you know? It was scary."

Gaia felt as if she'd just swallowed something too hot too fast. But she shook it off. This was not possible. Oliver was Oliver now. But Sam's green eyes were pleading with her, begging her to believe him—maybe even to help him. And why not? He was terrified of being imprisoned again. Or worse.

Suddenly Gaia knew that she'd done the wrong

thing when she'd sent Sam to meet with Oliver. It was all there again—right on the surface—the hopeless hours, the beatings, the agony of being caged up like a worthless animal. Sam looked tortured again. She felt it within her own heart.

"Sam. . . I. . . I'm so sorry," Gaia said. "I shouldn't have made you go."

"It doesn't matter," Sam told her. He reached for her hands and held them both in hers. Gaia resisted the urge to look toward the living room. What would Jake think if he saw this? "It doesn't matter," Sam repeated. "I just wanted to warn you. Loki's back. You have to do something. You have to protect yourself."

The sincerity behind his concern touched Gaia, but she knew it was unfounded. She was safe now. They all were. Sam had to get used to it as she had.

"Sam, it's going to be okay," Gaia said. "Nothing's going to happen to you."

Sam took a deep breath and looked at the floor. "You don't believe me, do you?"

"I. . . can't," Gaia said.

"Fine," Sam said, nodding. He pressed his lips together and lifted his eyes to meet hers. "Just be careful."

Then he reached out and touched her cheek, his palm cupping her face. Gaia's skin tingled with warmth. Seconds later he was gone, walking off down the hall. She waited until she heard the front door close before rejoining Jake in the living room.

"What was that all about?" Jake asked flatly.

"Nothing," Gaia told him. "He just wanted to make sure I was okay."

"Isn't that my job now?" Jake asked, point-blank. No double-talk. No games.

"It's always kind of been *my* job," Gaia told him.

Jake cracked a smile, reached out, and grabbed her hand. He pulled her down onto the couch and into his side.

"Well, now you have an assistant," he said, laying his arm on top of hers.

Jake's attitude toward Sam was comforting. He wasn't going to walk out on her for having a past that kept rearing its dramatic head. Jake Montone could take it.

"So, are we going to watch this movie or what? I hate late fees." He picked up the remote again. Gaia sighed and allowed her cheek to lean into his chest. As ridiculously tricked-out cars screeched across the screen, she told herself to forget about Sam. He'd readjust. He'd be okay. And so would she. They would all be just fine.

It was time to stop dwelling on other people's feelings. It was time to stop thinking about what might happen tomorrow or next week or next month. For the first time she could remember, life and all its possibilities were open to her.

Gaia Moore was ready to start living.

```
        Things I have:
    A father
    An uncle
    A maybe boyfriend
    A home
    A future


        Things I don't have:
    Fear
    A grandfather (at least not one
I will ever acknowledge)
    Psychos tracking my every move
    Uncertainty


For once the scales have
tipped in my favor. And life is
good.
    Life
    Is
    Good.
```

here is a
sneak peek of
Fearless™ #31:
NORMAL

This giddy lovesick child thing was going to give her a **hypnosis** goddamn ulcer.

a mild form of

THERE WAS NOTHING IN THE WORLD

Disgustingly Normal

more disgustingly normal than lunch at the Village School cafeteria. And Gaia was all about disgustingly normal. Because, secretly, she wasn't finding it so disgusting anymore. Of course, the food was just as hideous as ever, as in today's "Thing with Egg in Yellow Sauce." And of course, the majority of the company was just as hideous as ever, as in a table full of overdressed FOHs squawking their deafening tribal squawks like a pack of hungry emus. But in just the last week, Gaia had somehow grown accustomed to successfully blocking out the majority of nauseating stimuli in the cafeteria. Perhaps it had something to do with the new habit that had just started to form—a habit Gaia was beginning to share with Jake Montone.

For the past week, they had both been plowing their way through the first three classes of the day and then rushing to the cafeteria, often knocking down passersby, to meet up for their first real chunk of time together. Disgustingly normal.

Without really noticing, Gaia tugged a plate of Thing with Egg onto her tray, and one of anything else her hand happened to grab on the cafeteria line. Her head was turned nearly a hundred and eighty degrees behind her back, her eyes scanning across the entire lunchroom full of freaks and freaks disguised as non-freaks, searching for her first Jake glimpse of the day. She had boiled it down to a routine procedure at this point. Step one: Look for the thick dark hair among the sea of platinum blonds and backward baseball caps. Step two: Look for the smooth olive skin among all the haggard, greasy, pale-skinned New Yorkers. And if all else failed, step three: Check for that confident swagger that used to annoy the living crap out of her. Actually, it still annoyed the living crap out of her. But in a good way. That was the weirdest part of this new "thing" she was having with Jake. All his most annoying qualities were suddenly so. . . endearing. His karate jock posturing, his "I'm a handsome man" smile, his too-tight T-shirts—they all used to make her sick, but now she could just see them for what they were: covers.

They were all just covers. Just like everyone else milling around that lunchroom. Pick your cliché, act like it and dress like it, and you'd gotten a clear-cut identity for the world to relate to. No one would ever have to dig too deep to make a connection. No one would ever have to find out what a complicated, lost, clueless soul you really were. Mike Shelton, for example, simplified his life by dying his hair platinum and adding the word *dude* before and after every sentence. This way, no one would ever wonder what he was thinking, because they would assume he was far too stupid to be thinking anything. Even the FOHs exaggerated their dumbness so as to keep from intimidating attractive men with low self-esteem. And Gaia, in her own way, wasn't really any better. Even she tended to hide behind her fearless angry scowl and her rumpled sixth-grade-boy wardrobe.

But if Jake was willing to see past her personal clichés, the least she could do was provide him the same courtesy. Conceited karate jock was his cover. And of all the covers to have, Gaia had to admit that Jake's wasn't altogether physically unattractive. Okay, it was mildly arousing.

Okay, not mildly. Not anymore. Nothing about Jake was *mildly* anything anymore. Everything was now falling into the category of extremely and absolutely and even unbearably. The painfully good kind of unbearably.

Gaia looked further to the back of the room, searching for Jake, when she felt a sudden pang of complex emotions jabbing at her heart and pricking her spine. This was another feeling she had grown accustomed to lately. It was the feeling of spotting Ed Fargo in school.

Ed and Kai were sitting across from each other at one of the smaller tables in the back, and Gaia's eyes had just met Ed's by accident. It was the kind of moment she and Ed both worked very hard to avoid in this little bread box of a school. It was at moments like these that Gaia found herself wishing very badly that she went to one of those giganto, super-homogenized, ultra-conglomerated suburban high schools with five thousand students and multiple buildings that looked like bad science fiction sets. Then she and Ed could probably go for months without running into each other even once. But here in the intimate universe of VCS they had no such luck.

The glimpse of Ed was particularly weird for Gaia as she had just been in the middle of an embarrassingly dreamy Jake moment. Too weird. Weird for way too many reasons. The moment, of course, lasted less than a second, as Gaia quickly focused in every other direction she could find (as most likely did Ed).

That was the standard now between Gaia and Ed. Distance. Distance and avoidance. But Gaia still felt like such an extraterrestrial whenever she let herself think about it for too long. How could two people who had been so utterly and completely in love now be going out of their way to avoid anything more than a second's worth of eye contact? But once again she had to remind herself: That was normal. That kind of thing happened all the time in the world of normal people. Avoidance was all she and Ed could muster now. So fine. Avoidance it would be.

Gaia did her best to dump the little pangs of jealousy she was feeling about Ed and Kai. Not just because watching them together made her stomach mildly ill, but because it was such a ridiculously unfair double standard. Here she was, rushing to the cafeteria for another rendezvous with Jake, so what right did she have to be even the least bit resentful of Ed and Kai? None. She had no right whatsoever. Because this was the deal now. This was how things worked. Ed and Kai over there, and Gaia and Jake over here. . .

Gaia and Jake. . . She ran the phrase through her head again. *Gaia and Jake. . . Is it "Gaia and Jake" now? Is that what we call it?*

"Twenty-one seconds."

Jake's smooth, deep voice was only inches from her ear. The rest of the human race would have been startled by a voice so close sneaking up from behind, but not Gaia. She merely turned her head to look behind her, letting her eyes drift up from his lips to the contrast of his white teeth set against his olive skin, to his eyes. She liked Jake's eyes. Even when she'd first met him and thought he was a macho asshole, she'd liked his eyes. She just hadn't been ready to admit it to herself.

"What?" she asked, letting the Ed moment drift away into space as her entire focus settled on `Jake's clear green irises.`

"Twenty-one seconds," Jake repeated, holding a tray in one hand as he tossed two sandwiches on it and then grabbed Gaia's hand. "I could have made it here in nineteen, but this freshman with an astronomy project was blocking the third-floor doorway."

Jake pulled Gaia with him to a seat by the window, dropped both their trays down, and then plopped down across the table from her.

And then the staring started.

This was part of the daily ritual as well. Rush to the cafeteria, find each other, grab a table, and then a few moments of awkwardly intense staring that continued to leave Gaia with an inexplicable rush of blood to the center of her chest. She always tried to pass it off as more of a staring *contest*, but she had a feeling that Jake could see past her competitive veneer.

Jake was the first to break the silence today. He leaned his head slightly forward across the table and lowered his voice. "How freakin' weird is this?" he said with a subversive little smile.

"How weird is what?" Gaia asked, feeling an unexpected tinge of insecurity. Was he talking about them? Weird that they kept meeting in the lunchroom like lovesick little kids? Weird that they'd been making goo-goo eyes at each other? Weird that they were even hanging out like this at all? It *was* weird, wasn't it? It was so out of nowhere. But Gaia had thought it was *good* weird. Didn't Jake think it was good weird?

Jesus, will you listen to yourself? No, on second thought she didn't want to listen to herself. It was all far too embarrassing. Even if she was the only one hearing it inside her own head.

"This," Jake said with a smile. "Us. Here. Like this. Weird."

"What's weird about it?" Gaia said, far too defensively. She felt her spine stiffen. "I don't see anything weird about it, we're just. . . I mean, whatever. *You're* weird. . . ."

"Whoa," Jake laughed, squeezing Gaia's hand. "I meant *good* weird."

"Oh." Her posture started to relax again. Maybe she had been burned by this boy-girl thing one too many times. Her eyes darted momentarily toward Ed's table, and then she trained them back on Jake. "Okay," she said with a half smile. "Good weird is good. I'm fine with good weird." She squeezed her hand tighter around Jake's thick knuckles, and shook off her unexpected mini–freak-out.

"I mean, I don't know," Jake mused, leaning even closer. "I kind of feel like we're our secret identities in school or something. You know what I mean?"

Gaia scrunched her eyes with confusion. "Um. . . No. Not really."

Jake glanced on either side of him to check for eavesdroppers. "You *know*," he said. "I mean, when we're out there in Siberia, or we're dealing with Yuri, then it's like we're two—"

"Jake," Gaia interrupted, scolding him slightly with her eyes.

Jake's eyes widened in response. "What?" he asked innocently.

"We don't talk about that stuff when we're at school," she explained quietly. "In fact, we try not to talk about it at all."

"*Exactly.*" He smiled. "Like I said, it's like we're our secret identities. I don't know, I just think it's kind of cool—your life, Oliver's life, taking down all those sons of bitches out there and then coming back here and wondering what's for lunch—"

"No, it's *not* cool," Gaia snapped in a loud whisper. She had to make sure she had Jake's full attention. "Believe me, Jake, there's nothing *cool* about it, and there's nothing *fun* about it. It's a freakin' nightmare is what it is. It's torture, that's what it is. *This* is the good part, Jake. You and me sitting here having our lunches in the cafeteria like everybody else. That's the cool thing. Not all that other miserable crap."

Jake had pretty much been scolded into silence.

Gaia immediately felt guilty for ruining their perfectly lovely moment here at the table, but she needed to make sure her point would sink in. There was nothing remotely cool about nearly dying every few days. And if Gaia'd had any choice in the matter—if she hadn't been genetically incapable of chickening out and running away; if she weren't always the unsuspecting object of someone's plots and schemes and obsessions, then she would have been delighted to never engage in another spy game or pathetic street brawl for as long as she lived.

"Okay," Jake said. "I'm sorry."

The longer Gaia stared into his wide open eyes, the guiltier she felt. "No," she said, dipping her head for a moment. "No, I'm sorry, I just. . . I. . ."

Okay, honest or not honest? The question rushed through Gaia's head repeatedly as her mouth hung half-open in midsentence. *Honest or the classic Gaia clam-up when things get remotely deep? New Gaia. . . What does New Gaia do in this situation?*

New Gaia would be honest. New Gaia wouldn't clam up and mess with Jake's trust like she'd messed with Sam's and Ed's.

"I just have these. . . issues," Gaia forced herself to say. "Issues about boys getting involved in my life like that. . . and I just. . . Look, I don't know if you've noticed, Jake, but I'm a little screwed up, okay?"

Jake smiled and then leaned to meet her at the center of the table. "You know, for someone so brave. . . you sure worry a lot." That was oddly true, she supposed. "If you don't want to talk about that stuff, we don't have to," he went on. "But doesn't that get kind of lonely after a while? Don't you think there's something kind of cool about having someone to go through it all with? I mean *all* of it, not just half of it. I don't know. . . . I like being there for all of it. . . or whatever. Forget it."

Jake shrugged his shoulders and took a massive

bite of his sandwich. But Gaia just sat there staring at him as he chewed. The truth was. . . yes, she liked having someone there for all of it. Yes, she did. She liked having Jake next to her in a fight. She liked having him next to her at lunch. She liked having him next to her.

"What?" he asked defensively, looking at her again. "What? I take big bites. I trained hard this morning. I'm hungry."

"What? No," Gaia assured him. "No, nothing. I wasn't—"

"What was that look?"

"What? I was just. . ." Gaia found her hands reaching behind her head and fiddling with her hair. She readjusted her ponytail, but it only made the hair fall further into her face. "Nothing, just. . ." *Honest. New Gaia is going to talk more.* "It's not a *bad* look," she explained. "I was. . . I liked what you just said. . . . Whatever." *This is not talking more. This is stammering like an idiot.* "This is me *happy*, okay?" she announced. She practically slapped Jake in the face with the words, but at least she'd managed to get them out of her mouth. "I mean, this is what I look like when I'm. . . happy."

A grin began to spread across Jake's face. A wide, pearly white, excessively hot, excessively confident grin.

"Stop it," Gaia warned, trying to suppress the embarrassed smile that was about to pop up on her own face. This giddy lovesick child thing was going to give her a goddamn ulcer.

"Stop what?" Jake asked, his smile widening as he tried to regain her eye contact, which was difficult given the fact that her hand was beginning to involuntarily mask her eyes.

"*Stop it*," she muttered between clenched teeth, "or I swear to God, I will mash your face against this table and that grin will be forever altered." Gaia collected herself and tried to look back in Jake's eyes, but his smile had only grown larger. "Eat your freaking sandwich, Jake, or I will never say anything nice *again*."

Jake leaned toward her. "We need to talk," he announced with a smile. He locked his eyes so tightly and securely with hers that she did not even try to avert his glance this time. It was almost like a mild form of hypnosis.

"About what?" Gaia uttered.

"Later," he said. "I have to go meet my dad for lunch, actually. But we're going to move your stuff over to that boarding house tonight, right?"

"Right. . . ?"

"So I'll find you after school. And we'll walk. And we'll talk."

"About *what*?" Gaia repeated. But of course some part of her was smarter than that. She could see in his eyes what he wanted to talk about. He wanted to talk about *them*. He wanted to talk about what was clearly happening between them and what was *going* to happen between them. He wanted to talk about when talking would not be what they spent most of their time doing. He wanted to talk about everything Gaia had been having a delightful time *not* talking about. But exactly how long was she planning to avoid that talk? Old Gaia would vote for as long as humanly possible, given how ridiculously burned she'd been with all this romantic stuff. But New Gaia. . . ? What would New Gaia do?

"Not here," Jake said. "Later. After school. We'll talk. Okay? You and me."

Gaia looked deeper in his eyes. "Okay," she heard herself say.

"Okay," he said. And before he'd even finished that one word, he'd pressed his large hands against the table, leaned his entire torso across it, and kissed her. Short, sweet, and deep on the lips. In the middle of the lunchroom. With the entire class looking on.

It was so unexpected. And yet it was so natural. As if it belonged. As if they'd been together for months. And for that one moment, Gaia felt like they had been. She felt like everything was right. She felt undeniably normal. For one perfect moment, with Jake's lips pressed to hers, she felt like one of those real girls, complete with real-girl tingles down the back of her neck, and her real-girl hands clasped tightly to her seat. And just as quickly, Jake pulled away, backing out of the lunchroom as he smiled at her.

"After school," he repeated. Jake's exit would have been excessively smooth, but he bumped into a sophomore girl as he backed his way out, nearly smashing her entire tray of Thing with Egg into her chest.

So much for confident swagger.